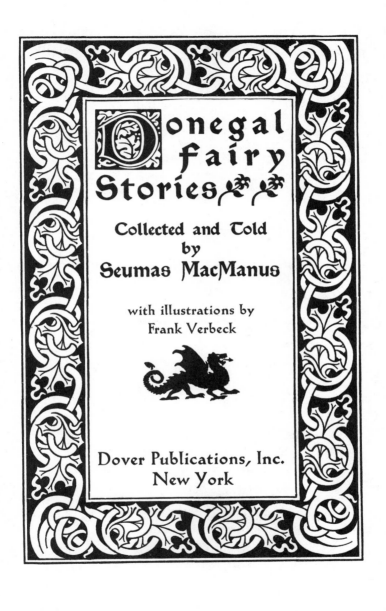

Donegal Fairy Stories

Collected and Told
by
Seumas MacManus

with illustrations by
Frank Verbeck

Dover Publications, Inc.
New York

This Dover edition, first published in 1968, is an
unabridged and unaltered republication of the work
originally published by McClure, Phillips & Co. in
1900.

Library of Congress Catalog Card Number: 68-28406

Manufactured in the United States of America
Dover Publications, Inc.
180 Varick Street
New York, N. Y. 10014

Is veisciobal úṁal a ṫoirbireas, le ur-
raim ṁóir, an leabairín beag so
vo ċuiṁne na seanċuive gaeveal-
aċ sin vo ċongḃuiġ beó vúinn
ꞇre gráv ꞇíre agus gráv
sgéalaigeaċꞇa aṁáin
sean sgéalꞇa breáġa
ár gciniv, ó aois go
h-aois agus ó
ġlúin go
glún.

It is a humble disciple who dedicates with
great reverence this little book to the
memory of those Gaelic shanachies
who have kept alive for us—
through love of country and
love of story-telling only
—the fine ancient tales
of our race, from age
to age and from
generation to
generation.

TABLE OF CONTENTS

Our Tales

TALES as old as the curlew's call are to-day listened to around the hearths of Donegal with the same keen and credulous eagerness with which they were hearkened to hundreds of years ago. Of a people whose only wealth is mental and spiritual, the thousand such tales are not the least significant heritage. Of those tales, the ten following are but the lightest.

The man who brings his shaggy pony to the forge "reharses a rale oul' tale" for the boys, whilst he lazily works the bellows for Dan.

As she spins in the glow of the fir-blaze on the long winter nights, the old white-capped woman, with hair like a streak of lint, holds the fireside circle spellbound with such tales as these.

Our Tales

When at Taig, the tailor's, on a Saturday night, an exasperated man clamors angrily for the long-promised coat, Taig says, "Arrah, Conal, man, have sense, and be quate, and sit down till ye hear a wondherful story of anshint happenin's." And the magic of the tale restores Conal to a Christian frame of mind, and sends him home forgetful of a great procrastinator's deceit.

When the beggarman, coming in at dayli'gone, drops his staff and sheds his bags in token that he deigns to honor the good people with his presence for that night, among young and old there is anticipative joy for the grand stories with which he will certainly enchant them till (too soon) *an bhean-an-tighe* shakes her beads and says it is rosary-time.

The professional shanachy recites them to a charmed audience in the wake-house, in the potato field, on the green hillside on summer Sundays, and at the cross-roads in blissful autumn gloamings, whilst the green marge rests his hearers' aching limbs.

Like generations of his people, one particular barefoot boy, being himself enchanted with them, longed to transmit their charm to others, and spent many, many delightful hours acquiring fresh ones, and recounting old ones to groups

Our Tales

the most sceptical of whom more than half believed, like himself, in their literal truth. To a wider world and more cultured, he would fain tell them now. He would wish that this world might hear of the wonderful happenings with our ears, and see them with our eyes, and consent to experience for a few hours the charmed delight with which our simple, kindly people, at the feet of their own shanachies, hearken to them. He would wish that this world might, for a few hours, give him their credence on trust, consent to forget temporarily that life is hard and joyless, be foolish, simple children once more, and bring to the entertainment the fresh and fun-loving hearts they possessed ere the world's wisdom came to them.

And if they return to the world's wise ways with a lurking delight in their hearts, the shanachy will again feel rejoiced and proud for the triumph of our grand old tales.

SEUMAS MACMANUS.

Donegal, Old Lammas Day, 1900.

The Plaisham

The Plaisham

NANCY and Shamus were man and wife, and they lived all alone together for forty years; but at length a good-for-nothing streel of a fellow named Rory, who lived close by, thought what a fine thing it would be if Shamus would die, and he could marry Nancy, and get the house, farm, and all the stock. So he up and said to Nancy:

"What a pity it is for such a fine-looking woman as you to be bothered with that ould, complainin', good-for-nothing crony of a man that's as full of pains and aches as an egg's full of meat. If you were free of him the morrow, the finest and handsomest young man in the parish would be proud to have you for a wife."

At first Nancy used to laugh at this; but at

last, when he kept on at it, it began to prey on Nancy's mind, and she said to young Rory one day : "I don't believe a word of what you say. Who would take me if Shamus was buried the morra ?"

"Why," says Rory, "you'd have the pick of the parish. I'd take you myself."

"Is that true?" says Nancy.

"I pledge you my word," says Rory, "I would."

"Oh, well, even if you would yourself," says Nancy, "Shamus won't be buried to-morrow, or maybe, God help me, for ten years to come yet."

"You've all that in your own hands," says Rory.

"How's that ?" says Nancy.

"Why, you can kill him off," says Rory.

"I wouldn't have the ould crature's blood on my head," says Nancy.

"Neither you need," says Rory.

And then he sat down and began to tell Nancy how she could do away with Shamus and still not have his blood on her head.

Now there was a prince called Connal, who lived in a wee sod house close by Nancy and Shamus, but whose fathers before him, ere their

The Plaisham

money was wasted, used to live in a grand
castle. So, next day, over Nancy goes to this
prince, and to him says : "Why, Prince Connal,
isn't it a shame to see the likes of you livin' in
the likes of that house ? "

"I know it is," said he, "but I cannot do any
better."

"Botheration," says Nancy, "you easily
can."

"I wish you would tell me how," says Prince
Connal.

"Why," says Nancy, "there's my Shamus
has little or nothing to do, an' why don't you
make him build you a castle ? "

"Ah," says the prince, laughing, "sure, Shamus couldn't build me a castle."

Says Nancy : "You don't know Shamus, for
there's not a thing in the wide world he couldn't
do if he likes to ; but he's that lazy, that if you
don't break every bone in his body to make him
do it, he won't do it."

"Is that so ? " says Prince Connal.

"That's so," says Nancy. "So if you order
Shamus to build you a castle an' have it up in
three weeks, or that you'll take his life if he
doesn't, you'll soon have a grand castle to live
in," says she.

5

Donegal Fairy Stories

"Well, if that's so," says Prince Connal, "I'll not be long wanting a castle."

So on the very next morning, over he steps to Shamus's, calls Shamus out, and takes him with him to the place he had marked out for the site of his castle, and shows it to Shamus, and tells him he wants him to have a grand castle built and finished on that spot in three weeks' time.

"But," says Shamus, says he, "I never built a castle in my life.   I know nothing about it, an' I couldn't have you a castle there in thirty-three years, let alone three weeks."

"O!" says the prince, says he, "I'm toul' there's no man in Ireland can build a castle better nor faster than you, if you only like to ; and if you haven't that castle built on that ground in three weeks," says he, "I'll have your life. So now choose for yourself."   And he walked away, and left Shamus standing there.

When Shamus heard this, he was a down-hearted man, for he knew that Prince Connal was a man of his word and would not stop at taking any man's life any more than he would from putting the breath out of a beetle.   So down he sits and begins to cry; and while Shamus was crying there, up to him comes a Wee Red Man, and says to Shamus: "What are you crying about ?"

The Plaisham

"Ah, my poor man," says Shamus, says he, "don't be asking me, for there's no use in telling you, you could do nothing to help me."

"You don't know that," says the Wee Red Man, says he. "It's no harm to tell me anyhow."

So Shamus, to relieve his mind, ups and tells the Wee Red Man what Prince Connal had threatened to do to him if he had not a grand castle finished on that spot in three weeks.

Says the little man, says he: "Go to the Fairies' Glen at moonrise the night, and under the rockin' stone at the head of the glen you'll find a white rod. Take that rod with you, and mark out the plan of the castle on this ground with it; then go back and leave the rod where you got it, and by the time you get back again your castle will be finished."

At moonrise that night Shamus, as you may be well assured, was at the rockin' stone at the head of the Glen of the Fairies, and from under it he got a little white rod. He went to the hill where the Prince's castle was to be built, and with the point of the rod he marked out the plan of the castle, and then he went back and left the rod where he got it.

The next morning, when Prince Connal got up

Donegal fairy Stories

out of bed and went out of his little sod hut to take the air, his eyes were opened, I tell you, to see the magnificent castle that was standing finished and with the coping-stones on it on the hill above. He lost no time till he went over to thank Shamus for building him such a beautiful castle ; and when Nancy heard that the castle was finished, it was she that was the angry woman.

She went out and looked at the castle, and she wondered and wondered, too, but she said nothing. She had a long chat with Rory that day again, and from Rory she went off to Prince Connal, and says she : "Now, didn't I tell you right well what Shamus could do ? "

"I see you did," says Prince Connal, "and it is very thankful to you I am. I'm contented now for life," says he, "and I'll never forget yourself and Shamus."

"Contented ! " says she ; "why, that place isn't half finished yet."

"How's that ? " says Prince Connal.

"Why," says she, "you need a beautiful river flowing past that castle, with lovely trees, and birds singing in the branches, and you should have the ocean roaring up beside it."

" But still," says Prince Connal, says he, " one

8

The Plaisham

can't have everything. This is a hundred miles from a river and a hundred miles from an ocean, and no trees ever grew on this hill, nor ever could grow on it, and no bird ever sang on it for the last three hundred years."

" Then all the more reason," says she, " why you should have all them things."

" But I can't have them," says Prince Connal.

" Can't you ? " says she. " Yes, you can. If you promise to have Shamus's life unless he has you all those things by your castle in three days, you'll soon have all you want," says Nancy.

"Well, well, that's wonderful," says Prince Connal, says he, " and I'll do it."

So he sets out, and goes to Shamus's house, and calls Shamus out to him to tell him that his castle was very bare-looking without something. about it. Says he : "Shamus, I want you to put a beautiful river flowing past it, with plenty of trees and bushes along the banks, and also birds singing in them; and I want you to have the ocean roaring up by it also."

" But, Prince Connal," says Shamus, says he, "you know very well that I couldn't get you them things."

" Right well I know you can," says Prince Connal, " and I'll give you three days to have

all them things done; and if you haven't them
done at the end of three days, then I'll have
your life." And away goes Prince Connal.

Poor Shamus, he sat down and began to cry
at this, because he knew that he could not do
one of these things. And as he was crying and
crying he heard a voice in his ear, and looking
up he saw the Wee Red Man.

"Shamus, Shamus," says he, "what's the
matter with you?"

"O," says Shamus, says he, "there's no use
in telling you what's the matter with me this
time. Although you helped me before, there's
not a man in all the world could do what I've
got to do now."

"Well, anyhow," says the Wee Red Man, "if
I can't do you any good, I'll do you no harm."

So Shamus, to relieve his mind, ups and
tells the Wee Red Man what's the matter with
him.

"Shamus," says the Wee Red Man, says he,
"I'll tell you what you'll do. When the moon's
rising to-night, be at the head of the Glen of the
Fairies, and at the spring well there you'll find a
cup and a leaf and a feather. Take the leaf and
the feather with you, and a cup of water, and
go back to the castle. Throw the water from

While Shamus was crying there, up to him comes a Wee Red Man.

The Plaisham

you as far as you can throw it, and then blow
the leaf off your right hand, and the feather off
your left hand, and see what you'll see."

Shamus promised to do this. And when the
moon rose that night, Shamus was at the spring
well of the Glen of the Fairies, and he found
there a cup, a leaf, and a feather. He lifted a
cup of water and took it with him, and the leaf
and the feather, and started for the castle. When
he came there, he pitched the cup of water from
him as far as he could pitch it, and at once the
ocean, that was a hundred miles away, came
roaring up beside the castle, and a beautiful river
that had been flowing a hundred miles on the
other side of the castle came flowing down past
it into the ocean. Then he blew the leaf off his
right hand, and all sorts of lovely trees and
bushes sprang up along the river banks. Then
he blew the feather off his left hand, and the
trees and the bushes were filled with all sorts
and varieties of lovely singing birds, that made
the most beautiful music he ever had heard.

And maybe that was not a surprise to Prince
Connal when he got up in the morning and
went out. Off he tramped to Shamus's to thank
Shamus and Nancy, and when Nancy heard this
she was the angry woman.

Donegal fairy Stories

That day she had another long confab with Rory, and from him she went off again to Prince Connal, and asked him how he liked his castle and all its surroundings.

He said he was a pleased and proud man, that he was thankful to her and her man, Shamus, and that he would never forget it to them the longest day of his life.

"O, but," says she, "you're not content. This night you'll have a great gathering of princes and lords and gentlemen feasting in your castle, and you'll surely want something to amuse them with. You must get a plaisham."

"What's a plaisham?" said Prince Connal.

"O," says Nancy, "it's the most wonderful and most amusing thing in the world; it will keep your guests in good humor for nine days and nine nights after they have seen it."

"Well," says Prince Connal, "that must be a fine thing entirely, and I'm sure I would be mighty anxious to have it. But," says he, "where would I get it or how would I get it?"

"Well," says Nancy, "that's easy. If you order Shamus to bring a plaisham to your castle by supper time this night, and promise to have his life if he hasn't it there, he'll soon get it for you."

Their eyes were opened to see the magnificent castle that was standing finished.

The Plaisham

"Well, if that's so," says Prince Connal, "I'll not be long wanting a plaisham."

So home went Nancy rejoicing this time, for she said to herself that poor old Shamus would not be long living now, because there was no such thing known in the whole wide world as a plaisham; and though Shamus might build castles, and bring oceans and rivers and trees and birds to them, all in one night, he could not get a thing that did not exist and was only invented by Rory.

Well, off to Shamus went Prince Connal without much loss of time, and called Shamus out of his little cabin. He told him he was heartily well pleased with all he had done for him. "But there's one thing more I want you to do, Shamus, and then I'll be content," says he. "This night I give a grand supper to the lords, ladies, and gentry of the country, and I want something to amuse them with; so at supper time you must bring me a plaisham."

"A plaisham! What's that?" says Shamus.

"I don't know," says Prince Connal.

"No more do I," says Shamus, "an' how do you expect me to fetch it to you then?"

"Well," says Prince Connal, says he, "this is all there is to be said about it—if you haven't a plaisham at my castle door at supper time the night, you'll be a dead man."

"O, O," says Shamus, says he, and sat down on the ditch and began to cry, while Prince Connal went off home.

"Shamus, Shamus," says a voice in his ears, "what are you cryin' about now?"

Poor Shamus lifted his head and looked around, and there beside him stood the Wee Red Man.

"O!" says Shamus, says he, "don't mind asking me," he says, "for it's no use in telling you what's the matter with me now. You may build a castle for me," says he, "and you may bring oceans and rivers to it, and trees and birds; but you couldn't do anything to help me now."

"How do you know that?" said the Wee Red Man.

"O, I know it well," says Shamus, says he, "you couldn't give me the thing that never was an' never will be!"

"Well," says the Wee Red Man, says he, "tell me what it is anyhow. If I can't do you any good, sure I can't do you any harm."

So, to relieve his mind, Shamus ups and tells him that Prince Connal had ordered him, within twenty-four hours, to have at his castle door a

He found the ring hanging
from one of the branches
of the sciog bush.

plaisham. "But," says Shamus, says he, "there never was such a thing as that."

"Sure enough," says the Wee Red Man, "there never was. But still, if Prince Connal wants it, we must try to get it for him. This night, Shamus," says the Wee Red Man, says he, "go to the head of the Glen of the Fairies, to the sciog bush [Fairy thorn], where you'll find a bone ring hanging on a branch of the thorn. Take it with you back home. When you get home, young Rory will be chatting with your wife in the kitchen. Don't you go in there, but go into the byre [cowshed], and put the ring in the cow's nose ; then lie quiet, and you'll soon have a plaisham to drive to Prince Connal's castle door."

Shamus thanked the Wee Red Man, and that night he went to the head of the Glen of the Fairies, and sure enough, he found the ring hanging from one of the branches of the sciog bush. He took it with him, and started for home. When he looked in through the kitchen window, there he saw Nancy and Rory sitting over the fire, chatting and confabbing about how they would get rid of him ; but he said nothing, only went into the byre. He put the ring into the brannet cow's nose, and as soon as the ring went into it, the cow began to kick and rear and create a great tendherary of a noise entirely. Then Shamus got in under some hay in the corner.

It was no time at all until Nancy was out to find what was wrong with the brannet cow. She struck the cow with her fist to quiet her, but when she hit her, her fist stuck to the cow, and she could not get away.

Rory had come running out after Nancy to help her, and Nancy called : " Rory, Rory, pull me away from the cow."

Rory got hold of her to pull her away, but as he did so his hands stuck to Nancy, and he could not get away himself.

Up then jumped Shamus from under the hay in the corner. " Hup, Hup ! " says Shamus, says he, " drive on the plaisham."

And out of the byre starts the cow with Nancy stuck to her, and Rory stuck to that, and heads toward the castle, with the cow rearing and rowting, and Nancy and Rory yelling and bawling. They made a terrible din entirely, and roused the whole countryside, who flocked out to see what was the matter.

Down past Rory's house the cow went, and Rory's mother, seeing him sticking to Nancy, ran out to pull him away ; but when she laid her

Everyone that got hold of it stuck to it.

The Plaisham

hand on Rory, she stuck to him; and "Hup,
Hup!" says Shamus, says he, "drive on the
plaisham."

So on they went. And Rory's father ran after
them to pull the mother away; but when he
laid his hands on the mother, he stuck to her;
and "Hup, Hup!" says Shamus, "drive on the
plaisham."

On again they went, and next they passed
where a man was cleaning out his byre. When
the man saw the ridiculous string of them, he
flung a graip [fork] and a graipful of manure at
them, and it stuck to Rory's father; and "Hup,
Hup!" says Shamus, says he, "drive on the
plaisham." But the man ran after to save his
graip, and when he got hold of the graip, he
stuck to it; and "Hup, Hup!" says Shamus,
says he, "drive on the plaisham."

On they went; and a tailor came flying out of
his house with his lap-board in his hand. He
struck the string of them with the lap-board, the
lap-board stuck to the last man, and the tailor
stuck to it; and "Hup, Hup!" says Shamus,
says he, "drive on the plaisham."

Then they passed a cobbler's. He ran out
with his heel-stick, and struck the tailor; but the
heel-stick stuck to the tailor, and the cobbler

stuck to the heel-stick ; and " Hup, Hup ! " says Shamus, says he, " drive on the plaisham."

Then on they went, and they next passed a blacksmith's forge. The blacksmith ran out, and struck the cobbler with his sledge. The sledge stuck to the cobbler, and the blacksmith stuck to the sledge ; and " Hup, Hup ! " says Shamus, says he, " drive on the plaisham."

When they came near the castle, they passed a great gentleman's house entirely, and the gentleman came running out, and got hold of the blacksmith to pull him away ; but the gentleman stuck to the blacksmith, and could not get away himself ; and " Hup, Hup ! " says Shamus, says he, " drive on the plaisham."

The gentleman's wife, seeing him stuck, ran after her man to pull him away ; but the wife stuck to the gentleman ; and " Hup, Hup ! " says Shamus, says he, " drive on the plaisham."

Then their children ran after them to pull the mother away, and they stuck to the mother ; and "Hup, Hup ! " says Shamus, says he, "drive on the plaisham."

Then the butler ran to get hold of the children, and he stuck to them; and the footman ran to get hold of the butler, and stuck to him; and the cook ran to get hold of the footman, and stuck to

The Plaisham

him; and the servants all ran to get hold of the cook, and they stuck to her; and "Hup, Hup!" says Shamus, says he, "drive on the plaisham."

And on they went; and when they came up to the castle, the plaisham was a mile long, and the yelling and bawling and noise that they made could be heard anywhere within the four seas of Ireland. The racket was so terrible that Prince Connal and all his guests and all his servants and all in his house came running to the windows to see what was the matter, at all, at all; and when Prince Connal saw what was coming to his house, and heard the racket they were raising, he yelled to his Prime Minister to go and drive them off with a whip.

The Prime Minister ran meeting them, and took the whip to them; but the whip stuck to them, and he stuck to the whip; and "Hup, Hup!" says Shamus, says he, "drive on the plaisham."

Then Prince Connal ordered out all his other ministers and all of his servants to head it off and turn it away from his castle; but every one of the servants that got hold of it stuck to it; and "Hup, Hup!" says Shamus, says he, "drive on the plaisham."

And the plaisham moved on still for the castle.

Donegal fairy Stories

Then Prince Connal himself, with all his guests, ran out to turn it away ; but when Prince Connal laid hands on the plaisham, he stuck to it; and when his guest laid hands on him, they stuck one by one to him ; and "Hup, Hup !" says Shamus, says he, "drive on the plaisham."

And with all the racket and all the noise of the ranting, roaring, rearing, and rawting, in through the castle hall-door drove the plaisham, through and through and out at the other side. The castle itself fell down and disappeared, the bone ring rolled away from the cow's nose, and the plaisham all at once broke up, and when Prince Connal looked around, there was no castle at all, only the sod hut, and he went into it a sorry man.

And all the others slunk off home, right heartily ashamed of themselves, for the whole world was laughing at them. Nancy, she went east; and Rory, he went west; and neither one of them was ever heard of more. As for Shamus, he went home to his own little cabin, and lived all alone, happy and contented, for the rest of his life, and may you and I do the same.

The Amadan of the Dough

The Amadan of the Dough

THERE was a king once on a time that had a son that was an Amadan [half-foolish fellow]. The Amadan's mother died, and the king married again.

The Amadan's step-mother was always afraid of him beating her children, he was growing so big and strong. So to keep him from growing and to weaken him, she had him fed on dough made of raw meal and water, and for that he was called '' The Amadan of the Dough.'' But instead of getting weaker, it was getting stronger the Amadan was on this fare, and he was able to thrash all of his step-brothers together.

At length his step-mother told his father that he would have to drive the Amadan away. The father consented to put him away; but the Amadan refused to go till his father would give him a sword so sharp that it would cut a pack of wool falling on it.

Donegal Fairy Stories

After a great deal of time and trouble the father got such a sword and gave it to the Amadan; and when the Amadan had tried it and found it what he wanted, he bade them all goodby and set off.

For seven days and seven nights he traveled away before him without meeting anything wonderful, but on the seventh night he came up to a great castle. He went in and found no one there, but he found a great dinner spread on the table in the hall. So to be making the most of his time, down the Amadan sat at the table and whacked away.

When he had finished with his dinner, up to the castle came three young princes, stout, strong, able fellows, but very, very tired, and bleeding from wounds all over them.

They struck the castle with a flint, and all at once the whole castle shone as if it were on fire.

The Amadan sprang at the three of them to kill them. He said, "What do you mean by putting the castle on fire?"

"O Amadan," they said, "don't interfere with us, for we are nearly killed as it is. The castle isn't on fire. Every day we have to go out to fight three giants—Slat Mor, Slat Marr and Slat Beag. We fight them all day long, and just as

The Amadan of the Dough

night is falling we have them killed. But however it comes, in the night they always come to
life again, and if they didn't see this castle lit
up, they'd come in on top of us and murder
us while we slept. So every night, when we
come back from the fight, we light up the castle.
Then we can sleep in peace until morning, and
in the morning go off and fight the giants
again.

When the Amadan heard this, he wondered;
and he said he would very much like to help
them kill the giants. They said they would be
very glad to have such a fine fellow's help; and
so it was agreed that the Amadan should go with
them to the fight next day.

Then the three princes washed themselves and
took their supper, and they and the Amadan
went to bed.

In the morning all four of them set off, and
traveled to the Glen of the Echoes, where they
met the three giants.

"Now," says the Amadan, "if you three will
engage the two smaller giants, Slat Marr and Slat
Beag, I'll engage Slat Mor myself and kill him."

They agreed to this.

Now the smallest of the giants was far bigger
and more terrible than anything ever the Amadan

had seen or heard of in his life before, so you can fancy what Slat Mor must have been like.

But the Amadan was little concerned at this. He went to meet Slat Mor, and the two of them fell to the fight, and a great, great fight they had. They made the hard ground into soft, and the soft into spring wells ; they made the rocks into pebbles, and the pebbles into gravel, and the gravel fell over the country like hailstones. All the birds of the air from the lower end of the world to the upper end of the world, and all the wild beasts and tame from the four ends of the earth, came flocking to see the fight; and in the end the Amadan ran Slat Mor through with his sword and laid him down dead.

Then he turned to help the three princes, and very soon he laid the other two giants down dead for them also.

Then the three princes said they would all go home. The Amadan told them to go, but warned them not to light up the castle this night, and said he would sit by the giants' corpses and watch if they came to life again.

The three princes begged of him not to do this, for the three giants would come to life, and then he, having no help, would be killed.

The Amadan was angry with them, and or-

He sat down by the giants'
corpses to watch their coming to life again.

The Amadan of the Dough

dered them off instantly. Then he sat down by the giants' corpses to watch. But he was so tired from his great day's fighting that by and by he fell asleep.

About twelve o'clock at night, when the Amadan was sleeping soundly, up comes a cailliach [old hag] and four badachs [unwieldy big fellows], and the cailliach carried with her a feather and a bottle of iocshlainte [ointment of health], with which she began to rub the giants' wounds.

Two of the giants were already alive when the Amadan awoke, and the third was just opening his eyes. Up sprang the Amadan, and at him leaped them all—Slat Mor, Slat Marr, Slat Beag, the cailliach, and the four badachs.

If the Amadan had had a hard fight during the day, this one was surely ten times harder. But a brave and a bold fellow he was, and not to be daunted by numbers or showers of blows. They fought for long and long. They made the hard ground into soft, and the soft into spring wells; they made the rocks into pebbles, and the pebbles into gravel, and the gravel fell over the country like hailstones. All the birds of the air from the lower end of the world to the upper end of the world, and all the wild beasts and tame from the four ends of the earth, came flocking to see the fight; and one after the other of them the Amadan ran his sword through, until he had every one of them stretched on the ground, dying or dead.

And when the old cailliach was dying, she called the Amadan to her and put him under geasa [an obligation that he could not shirk] to lose the power of his feet, of his strength, of his sight, and of his memory if he did not go to meet and fight the Black Bull of the Brown Wood.

When the old hag died outright, the Amadan rubbed some of the iochslainte to his wounds with the feather, and at once he was as hale and as fresh as when the fight began. Then he took the feather and the bottle of iocshlainte, buckled on his sword, and started away before him to fulfil his geasa.

He traveled for the length of all that lee-long day, and when night was falling, he came to a little hut on the edge of a wood; and the hut had no shelter inside or out but one feather over it, and there was a rough, red woman standing in the door.

"You're welcome," says she, "Amadan of the Dough, the King of Ireland's son. What have you been doing or where are you going?"

The Amadan of the Dough

"Last night," says the Amadan, "I fought a great fight, and killed Slat Mor, Slat Marr, Slat Beag, the Cailliach of the Rocks, and four bad-achs. Now I'm under geasa to meet and to fight the Black Bull of the Brown Wood. Can you tell me where to find him?"

"I can that," says she, "but it's now night. Come in and eat and sleep."

So she spread for the Amadan a fine supper, and made a soft bed, and he ate heartily and slept heartily that night.

In the morning she called him early, and she directed him on his way to meet the Black Bull of the Brown Wood. "But my poor Amadan," she said, "no one has ever yet met that bull and come back alive."

She told him that when he reached the place of meeting, the bull would come tearing down the hill like a hurricane. "Here's a cloak," says she, "to throw upon the rock that is standing there. You hide yourself behind the rock, and when the bull comes tearing down, he will dash at the cloak, and blind himself with the crash against the rock. Then you jump on the bull's back and fight for life. If, after the fight, you are living, come back and see me; and if you are dead, I'll go and see you."

Donegal Fairy Stories

The Amadan took the cloak, thanked her, and set off, and traveled on and on until he came to the place of meeting.

When the Amadan came there, he saw the Bull of the Brown Wood come tearing down the hill like a hurricane, and he threw the cloak on the rock and hid behind it, and with the fury of his dash against the cloak the bull blinded himself, and the roar of his fury split the rock.

The Amadan lost no time jumping on his back, and with his sword began hacking and slashing him ; but he was no easy bull to conquer, and a great fight the Amadan had. They made the hard ground into soft, and the soft into spring wells ; they made the rocks into pebbles, and the pebbles into gravel, and the gravel fell over the country like hailstones. All the birds of the air from the lower end of the world to the upper end of the world, and all the wild beasts and tame from the four ends of the earth, came flocking to see the fight; at length, after a long time, the Amadan ran his sword right through the bull's heart, and the bull fell down dead. But before he died he put the Amadan under geasa to meet and to fight the White Wether of the Hill of the Waterfalls.

He threw the cloak on the
rock and hid behind it.

The Amadan of the Dough

Then the Amadan rubbed his own wounds with the iocshlainte, and he was as fresh and hale as when he went into the fight. Then he set out and traveled back again to the little hut that had no shelter without or within, only one feather over it, and the rough, red woman was standing in the door, and she welcomed the Amadan and asked him the news.

He told her all about the fight, and that the Black Bull of the Wood had put him under geasa to meet and to fight the White Wether of the Hill of the Waterfalls.

"I'm sorry for you, my poor Amadan," says she, "for no one ever before met that White Wether and came back alive. But come in and eat and rest anyhow, for you must be both hungry and sleepy."

So she spread him a hearty meal and made him a soft bed, and the Amadan ate and slept heartily; and in the morning she directed him to where he would meet the White Wether of the Hill of the Waterfalls. And she told him that no steel was tougher than the hide of the White Wether, that a sword was never yet made that could go through it, and that there was only one place— a little white spot just over the wether's heart— where he could be killed or sword could cut

43

through. And she told the Amadan that his only chance was to hit this spot.

The Amadan thanked her, and set out. He traveled away and away before him until he came to the Hill of the Waterfalls, and as soon as he reached it he saw the White Wether coming tearing toward him in a furious rage, and the earth he was throwing up with his horns was shutting out the sun.

And when the wether came up and asked the Amadan what great feats he had done that made him impudent enough to dare to come there, the Amadan said: "With this sword I have killed Slat Mor, Slatt Marr, Slatt Beag, the Cailliach of the Rocks and her four badachs, and likewise the Black Bull of the Brown Wood."

"Then," said the White Wether, "you'll never kill any other." And at the Amadan he sprang.

The Amadan struck at him with his sword, and the sword glanced off as it might off steel. Both of them fell to the fight with all their hearts, and such a fight never was before or since. They made the hard ground into soft, and the soft into spring wells ; they made the rocks into pebbles, and the pebbles into gravel, and the gravel fell over the country like hailstones. All the birds

The Amadan of the Dough

of the air from the lower end of the world to the upper end of the world, and all the wild beasts and tame from the four ends of the earth, came flocking to see the fight. But at length and at last, after a long and terrible fight, the Amadan seeing the little spot above the heart that the red woman had told him of, struck for it and hit it, and drove his sword through the White Wether's heart, and he fell down. And when he was dying, he called the Amadan and put him under a geasa to meet and fight the Beggarman of the King of Sweden.

The Amadan took out his bottle of iochslainte and rubbed himself with the iochslainte, and he was as fresh and hale as when he began the fight. Then he set out again, and when night was falling, he reached the hut that had no shelter within or without, only one feather over it, and the rough, red woman was standing in the door.

Right glad she was to see the Amadan coming back alive, and she welcomed him heartily and asked him the news.

He told her of the wonderful fight he had had, and that he was now under geasa to meet and fight the Beggarman of the King of Sweden.

She made him come in and eat and sleep, for

he was tired and hungry. And heartily the Amadan ate and heartily he slept; and in the morning she called him early, and directed him on his way to meet the Beggarman of the King of Sweden.

She told him that when he reached a certain hill, the beggarman would come down from the sky in a cloud; and that he would see the whole world between the beggarman's legs and nothing above his head. "If ever he finds himself beaten," she said, "he goes up into the sky in a mist, and stays there to refresh himself. You may let him go up once; but if you let him go up the second time, he will surely kill you when he comes down. Remember that. If you are alive when the fight is over, come to see me. If you are dead, I will go to see you."

The Amadan thanked her, parted with her, and traveled away and away before him until he reached the hill which she had told him of. And when he came there, he saw a great cloud that shot out of the sky, descending on the hill, and when it came down on the hill and melted away, there it left the Beggarman of the King of Sweden standing, and between his legs the Amadan saw the whole world and nothing over his head.

The Amadan of the Dough

And with a roar and a run the beggarman made for the Amadan, and the roar of him rattled the stars in the sky. He asked the Amadan who he was, and what he had done to have the impudence to come there and meet him.

The Amadan said : " They call me the Amadan of the Dough, and I have killed Slat Mor, Slat Marr, Slat Beag, the Cailliach of the Rocks and her four badachs, the Black Bull of the Brown Wood, and the White Wether of the Hill of the Waterfalls, and before night I'll have killed the Beggarman of the King of Sweden."

"That you never will, you miserable object," says the beggarman. "You're going to die now, and I'll give you your choice to die either by a hard squeeze of wrestling or a stroke of the sword."

"Well," says the Amadan, "if I have to die, I'd sooner die by a stroke of the sword."

"All right," says the beggarman, and drew his sword.

But the Amadan drew his sword at the same time, and both went to it. And if his fights before had been hard, this one was harder and greater and more terrible than the others put together. They made the hard ground into soft, and the soft into spring wells ; they made the rocks into pebbles, and the pebbles into gravel, and the gravel fell over the country like hail-stones. All the birds of the air from the lower end of the world to the upper end of the world, and all the wild beasts and tame from the four ends of the earth, came flocking to see the fight. And at length the fight was putting so hard upon the beggarman, and he was getting so weak, that he whistled, and the mist came around him, and he went up into the sky before the Amadan knew. He remained there until he refreshed himself, and then came down again, and at it again he went for the Amadan, and fought harder and harder than before, and again it was putting too hard on him, and he whistled as before for the mist to come down and take him up.

But the Amadan remembered what the red woman had warned him; he gave one leap into the air, and coming down, drove the sword through the beggarman's heart, and the beggar-man fell dead. But before he died he put geasa on the Amadan to meet and fight the Silver Cat of the Seven Glens.

The Amadan rubbed his wounds with the iocshlainte, and he was as fresh and hale as when he began the fight; and then he set out, and when night was falling, he reached the hut that

The Amadan of the Dough

had no shelter within or without, only one feather over it, and the rough, red woman was standing in the door.

Right glad she was to see the Amadan coming back alive, and she welcomed him right heartily, and asked him the news.

He told her that he had killed the beggarman, and said he was now under geasa to meet and fight the Silver Cat of the Seven Glens.

" Well," she said, " I'm sorry for you, for no one ever before went to meet the Silver Cat and came back alive. But," she says, "you're both tired and hungry ; come in and rest and sleep."

So in the Amadan went, and had a hearty supper and a soft bed; and in the morning she called him up early, and she gave him directions where to meet the cat and how to find it, and she told him there was only one vital spot on that cat, and it was a black speck on the bottom of the cat's stomach, and unless he could happen to run his sword right through this, the cat would surely kill him. She said :

" My poor Amadan, I'm very much afraid you'll not come back alive. I cannot go to help you myself or I would; but there is a well in my garden, and by watching that well I will know

how the fight goes with you. While there is
honey on top of the well, I will know you are
getting the better of the cat ; but if the blood
comes on top, then the cat is getting the better
of you ; and if the blood stays there, I will know,
my poor Amadan, that you are dead."

The Amadan bade her good-by, and set out to
travel to where the Seven Glens met at the sea.
Here there was a precipice, and under the precipice a cave. In this cave the Silver Cat lived,
and once a day she came out to sun herself on
the rocks.

The Amadan let himself down over the precipice by a rope, and he waited until the cat came
out to sun herself.

When the cat came out at twelve o'clock and
saw the Amadan, she let a roar out of her that
drove back the waters of the sea and piled them
up a quarter of a mile high, and she asked him
who he was and how he had the impudence to
come there to meet her.

The Amadan said : "They call me the Ama-
dan of the Dough, and I have killed Slat Mor,
Slat Marr, Slat Beag, the Cailliach of the Rocks
and her four badachs, the Black Bull of the Brown
Woods, the White Wether of the Hill of the
Waterfalls, and the Beggarman of the King of

The Cat came out and
asked the Amadan who
he was and how he had
the impudence to come
there to meet her.

The Amadan of the Dough

Sweden, and before night I will have killed the
Silver Cat of the Seven Glens."

"That you never will," says she, "for a dead
man you will be yourself." And at him she
sprang.

But the Amadan raised his sword and struck at
her, and both of them fell to the fight, and a
great, great fight they had. They made the hard
ground into soft, and the soft into spring wells ;
they made the rocks into pebbles, and the pebbles into gravel, and the gravel fell over the country like hailstones. All the birds of the air from
the lower end of the world to the upper end of
the world, and all the wild beasts and tame from
the four ends of the earth, came flocking to see
the fight; and if the fights that the Amadan had
had on the other days were great and terrible,
this one was far greater and far more terrible than
all the others put together, and the poor Amadan
sorely feared that before night fell he would be a
dead man.

The red woman was watching at the well in
her garden, and she was sorely distressed, for
though at one time the honey was uppermost,
at another time it was all blood, and again the
blood and the honey would be mixed; so she
felt bad for the poor Amadan.

Donegal Fairy Stories

At length the blood and the honey got mixed again, and it remained that way until night ; so she cried, for she believed the Amadan himself was dead as well as the Silver Cat.

And so he was. For when the fight had gone on for long and long, the cat, with a great long nail which she had in the end of her tail, tore him open from his mouth to his toes; and as she tore the Amadan open and he was about to fall, she opened her mouth so wide that the Amadan saw down to the very bottom of her stomach, and there he saw the black speck that the red woman had told him of. And just before he dropped he drove his sword through this spot, and the Silver Cat, too, fell over dead.

It was not long now till the red woman arrived at the place and found both the Amadan and the cat lying side by side dead. At this the poor woman was frantic with sorrow, but suddenly she saw by the Amadan's side the bottle of iocshlainte and the feather. She took them up and rubbed the Amadan with the iocshlainte, and he jumped to his feet alive and well, and fresh as when he began the fight.

He smothered her with kisses and drowned her with tears. He took the red woman with him, and set out on his journey back, and trav-

He smothered her with
kisses and drowned her
with tears.

The Amadan of the Dough

eled and traveled on and on till he came to the Castle of Fire.

Here he met the three young princes, who were now living happily with no giants to molest them. They had one sister, the most beautiful young maiden that the Amadan had ever beheld. They gave her to the Amadan in marriage, and gave her half of all they owned for fortune.

The marriage lasted nine days and nine nights. There were nine hundred fiddlers, nine hundred fluters, and nine hundred pipers, and the last day and night of the wedding were better than the first.

Conal and Donal and Taig

Conal and Donal and Taig

ONCE there were three brothers named Conal, Donal and Taig, and they fell out regarding which of them owned a field of land. One of them had as good a claim to it as the other, and the claims of all of them were so equal that none of the judges, whomsoever they went before, could decide in favor of one more than the other.

At length they went to one judge who was very wise indeed and had a great name, and every one of them stated his case to him.

He sat on the bench, and heard Conal's case and Donal's case and Taig's case all through, with very great patience. When the three of them had finished, he said he would take a day and a night to think it all over, and on the day after, when they were all called into court again, the

Donegal Fairy Stories

Judge said that he had weighed the evidence on all sides, with all the deliberation it was possible to give it, and he decided that one of them hadn't the shadow of a shade of a claim more than the others, so that he found himself facing the greatest puzzle he had ever faced in his life.

"But," says he, "no puzzle puzzles me long. I'll very soon decide which of you will get the field. You seem to me to be three pretty lazy-looking fellows, and I'll give the field to whichever of the three of you is the laziest."

"Well, at that rate," says Conal, "it's me gets the field, for I'm the laziest man of the lot."

"How lazy are you?" says the Judge.

"Well," said Conal, "if I were lying in the middle of the road, and there was a regiment of troopers come galloping down it, I'd sooner let them ride over me than take the bother of getting up and going to the one side."

"Well, well," says the Judge, says he, "you are a lazy man surely, and I doubt if Donal or Taig can be as lazy as that."

"Oh, faith," says Donal, "I'm just every bit as lazy."

"Are you?" says the Judge. "How lazy are you?"

"Well," said Donal, "if I was sitting right

Sooner let them ride over
me than take the trouble
of getting up.

Conal and Donal and Taig

close to a big fire, and you piled on it all the turf in a townland and all the wood in a barony, sooner than have to move I'd sit there till the boiling marrow would run out of my bones."

"Well," says the Judge, "you're a pretty lazy man, Donal, and I doubt if Taig is as lazy as either of you."

"Indeed, then," says Taig, "I'm every bit as lazy."

"How can that be?" says the Judge.

"Well," says Taig, "if I was lying on the broad of my back in the middle of the floor and looking up at the rafters, and if soot drops were falling as thick as hailstones from the rafters into my open eyes, I would let them drop there for the length of the lee-long day sooner than take the bother of closing the eyes."

"Well," says the Judge, "that's very wonderful entirely, and" says he, "I'm in as great a quandary as before, for I see you are the three laziest men that ever were known since the world began, and which of you is the laziest it certainly beats me to say. But I'll tell you what I'll do," says the Judge, "I'll give the field to the oldest man of you."

"Then," says Conal, "it's me gets the field."

Donegal Fairy Stories

"How is that ?" says the Judge ; "how old are you ?"

"Well, I'm that old," says Conal, "that when I was twenty-one years of age I got a shipload of awls and never lost nor broke one of them, and I wore out the last of them yesterday mending my shoes."

"Well, well," says the Judge, says he, "you're surely an old man, and I doubt very much that Donal and Taig can catch up to you."

" Can't I ?" says Donal ; "take care of that."

"Why," said the Judge, "how old are you ?"

"When I was twenty-one years of age," says Donal, "I got a shipload of needles, and yesterday I wore out the last of them mending my clothes."

"Well, well, well," says the Judge, says he, " you're two very, very old men, to be sure, and I'm afraid poor Taig is out of his chance anyhow."

"Take care of that," says Taig.

"Why," said the Judge, "how old are you, Taig ?"

Says Taig, "When I was twenty-one years of age I got a shipload of razors, and yesterday I had the last of them worn to a stump shaving myself."

Conal and Donal and Taig

"Well," says the Judge, says he, "I've often heard tell of old men," he says, "but anything as old as what you three are never was known since Methusalem's cat died. The like of your ages," he says, "I never heard tell of, and which of you is the oldest, that surely beats me to de‑cide, and I'm in a quandary again. But I'll tell you what I'll do," says the Judge, says he, "I'll give the field to whichever of you minds [remembers] the longest."

"Well, if that's it," says Conal, "it's me gets the field, for I mind the time when if a man tramped on a cat he usen't to give it a kick to console it."

"Well, well, well," says the Judge, "that must be a long mind entirely ; and I'm afraid, Conal, you have the field."

"Not so quick," says Donal, says he, "for I mind the time when a woman wouldn't speak an ill word of her best friend."

"Well, well, well," says the Judge, "your memory, Donal, must certainly be a very wonderful one, if you can mind that time. Taig," says the Judge, says he, "I'm afraid your memory can't compare with Conal's and Donal's."

"Can't it," says Taig, says he. "Take care

Donegal Fairy Stories

of that, for I mind the time when you wouldn't find nine liars in a crowd of ten men."

"Oh, Oh, Oh!" says the Judge, says he, "that memory of yours, Taig, must be a wonderful one." Says he : "Such memories as you three men have were never known before, and which of you has the greatest memory it beats me to say. But I'll tell you what I'll do now," says he; "I'll give the field to whichever of you has the keenest sight."

"Then," says Conal, says he, "it's me gets the field ; because," says he, "if there was a fly perched on the top of yon mountain, ten miles away, I could tell you every time he blinked."

"You have wonderful sight, Conal," says the Judge, says he, "and I'm afraid you've got the field."

"Take care," says Donal, says he, "but I've got as good. For I could tell you whether it was a mote in his eye that made him blink or not."

"Ah, ha, ha!" says the Judge, says he, "this is wonderful sight surely. Taig," says he, "I pity you, for you have no chance for the field now."

"Have I not?" says Taig. "I could tell you from here whether that fly was in good health or not by counting his heart beats."

Conal and Donal and Taig

" Well, well, well," says the Judge, says he,
"I'm in as great a quandary as ever. You are
three of the most wonderful men that ever I met,
and no mistake. But I'll tell you what I'll do,"
says he; " I'll give the field to the supplest man
of you."

" Thank you," says Conal. " Then the field is
mine."

" Why so?" says the Judge.

" Because," says Conal, says he, " if you filled
that field with hares, and put a dog in the middle
of them, and then tied one of my legs up my
back, I would not let one of the hares get out."

" Then, Conal," says the Judge, says he, " I
think the field is yours."

" By the leave of your judgeship, not yet," says
Donal.

" Why, Donal," says the Judge, says he,
" surely you are not as supple as that?"

" Am I not ?" says Donal. " Do you see that
old castle over there without door, or window,
or roof in it, and the wind blowing in and out
through it like an iron gate ?"

" I do," says the Judge. " What about that?"

"Well," says Donal, says he, " if on the storm-
iest day of the year you had that castle filled
with feathers, I would not let a feather be lost,

69

Donegal Fairy Stories

or go ten yards from the castle until I had caught and put it in again."

"Well, surely," says the Judge, says he, "you are a supple man, Donal, and no mistake. Taig," says he, "there's no chance for you now."

"Don't be too sure," says Taig, says he.

"Why," says the Judge, "you couldn't surely do anything to equal these things, Taig?"

Says Taig, says he: "I can shoe the swiftest race-horse in the land when he is galloping at his topmost speed, by driving a nail every time he lifts his foot."

"Well, well, well," says the Judge, says he, "surely you are the three most wonderful men that ever I did meet. The likes of you never was known before, and I suppose the likes of you will never be on the earth again. There is only one other trial," says he, "and if this doesn't decide, I'll have to give it up. I'll give the field," says he, "to the cleverest man amongst you."

"Then," says Conal, says he, "you may as well give it to me at once."

"Why? Are you that clever, Conal?" says the Judge, says he.

"I am that clever," says Conal, "I am that clever, that I would make a skin-fit suit of clothes

70

By driving a nail every
time he lifts a foot.

Conal and Donal and Taig

for a man without any more measurement than to tell me the color of his hair."

"Then, boys," says the Judge, says he, "I think the case is decided."

"Not so quick, my friend," says Donal, "not so quick."

"Why, Donal," says the Judge, says he, "you are surely not cleverer than that?"

"Am I not?" says Donal.

"Why," says the Judge, says he, "what can you do, Donal?"

"Why," says Donal, says he, "I would make a skin-fit suit for a man and give me no more measurement than let me hear him cough."

"Well, well, well," says the Judge, says he, "the cleverness of you two boys beats all I ever heard of. Taig," says he, "poor Taig, whatever chance either of these two may have for the field, I'm very, very sorry for you, for you have no chance."

"Don't be so very sure of that," says Taig, says he.

"Why," says the Judge, says he, "surely, Taig, you can't be as clever as either of them. How clever are you, Taig?"

"Well," says Taig, says he, "if I was a judge, and too stupid to decide a case that came up

73

Donegal Fairy Stories

before me, I'd be that clever that I'd look wise and give some decision."

"Taig," says the Judge, says he, "I've gone into this case and deliberated upon it, and by all the laws of right and justice, I find and decide that you get the field."

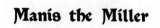

Manis the Miller

Manis the Miller

THERE was a man from the mountain, named Donal, once married the daughter of a stingy old couple who lived on the lowlands. He used to stay and work on his own wee patch of land all the week round, till it came to Saturday evening, and on Saturday evening he went to his wife's father's to spend Sunday with him.

Coming and going he always passed the mill of Manis, the miller, and Manis, who used to be watching him passing, always noticed, and thought it strange, that while he jumped the mill-race going to his wife's father's on a Saturday evening, he had always to wade through it coming back. And at last he stopped Donal one Monday morning, and asked him the meaning of it.

Donegal Fairy Stories

"Well, I'll tell you," says Donal, says he. "It's this: My old father-in-law is such a very small eater, that he says grace and blesses himself when I've only got a few pieces out of my meals ; so I'm always weak coming back on Monday morning."

Manis, he thought over this to himself for a while, and then says he : "Would you mind letting me go with you next Saturday evening? If you do, I promise you that you'll leap the mill-race coming back."

"I'll be glad to have you," says Donal.

Very well and good. When Saturday evening came, Manis joined Donal, and off they both trudged to Donal's father-in-law's.

The old man was not too well pleased at seeing Donal bringing a fresh hand, but Manis, he didn't pretend to see this, but made himself as welcome as the flowers in May. And when supper was laid down on Saturday night, Manis gave Donal the nudge, and both of them began to tie their shoes as if they had got loose, and they tied and tied away at their shoes, till the old man had eaten a couple of minutes, and then said grace and finished and got up from the table, thinking they wouldn't have the ill-manners to sit down after the meal was over.

Manis the Miller

But down to the table my brave Manis and Donal sat, and ate their hearty skinful. And when the old fellow saw this, he was gruff and grumpy enough, and it was little they could get out of him between that and bedtime.

But Manis kept a lively chat going, and told good stories, that passed away the night; and when bedtime came and they offered Manis a bed in the room, Manis said no, that there was no place he could sleep only one, and that was along the fireside.

The old man and the old woman both objected to this, and said they couldn't think of allowing a stranger to sleep there ; but all they could say or do wasn't any use, and Manis said he couldn't and wouldn't sleep in any other place, and insisted on lying down there, and lie down there he did in spite of them all, and they all went off to their beds.

But though Manis lay down, he was very careful not to let himself go to sleep ; and when he was near about two hours lying he hears the room door open easy, and the old woman puts her head out and listens, and Manis he snored as if he hadn't slept for ten days and ten nights before.

When the old woman heard this, she came on

up the floor and looked at him, and saw him like as if he was dead asleep. Then she hastened to put a pot of water on the fire, and began to make a pot of stir-about for herself and the old man, for this was the way, as Manis had well suspected, that they used to cheat Donal.

But just in the middle of the cooking of the pot of stir-about, doesn't Manis roll over and pretend to waken up? Up he sits, and rubs his eyes, and looks about him, and looks at the woman and at the pot on the fire.

"Ah," says he, "is it here ye are, or is it mornin' with ye?"

"Well, no," says she, "it isn't mornin', but we have a cow that's not well, and I had to put a mash on the fire here for her. I'm sorry I wakened ye."

"O, no, no!" says Manis, says he, "you haven't wakened me at all. It's this sore ankle I have here," says he, rubbing his ankle. "I've a very, very sore ankle," says he, "and it troubles me sometimes at night," he says, "and no matter how sound asleep I may be, it wakens me up, and I've got to sit up until I cure it." Says he: "There's nothin' cures it but soot—till I rub plenty of soot out of the chimney to it."

And Manis takes hold of the tongs, and he

Heard the door open easy.

Manis the Miller

begins pulling the soot down out of the chimney from above the pot, and for every one piece that fell on the fire, there were five pieces that fell into the pot. And when Manis thought he had the posset well enough spiced with the soot, he raised up a little of the soot from the fire and rubbed his ankle with it.

"And now," says he, "that's all right, and I'll sleep sound and not waken again till mornin'." And he stretched himself out again, and began to snore.

The old woman was pretty well vexed that she had had her night's work spoiled, and she went up to the room to the old man and told him what had happened to the stir-about. He got into a bad rage entirely, and asked her was Manis asleep again, and she said he was. Then he ordered her to go down and make an oat scowder * and put it on the ashes for him.

She went down, and got the oatmeal, and made a good scowder, and set it on the ashes, and then sat by it for the short while it would be doing.

But she hadn't it many minutes on the ashes when Manis let a cry out of him, as if it was in his sleep, and up he jumps and rubs his eyes

* A hastily baked oat-cake.

and looks about him ; and when he saw her, he said : "Och! is it here ye are? And I'm glad ye are," says he ; " because I've a great trouble on me mind, that's lying a load over me heart and wouldn't let me sleep, and I want to relieve me mind to ye," says Manis ; "an' then I'll sleep hearty and sound all the night after. I'll tell you the story," says he.

So he catches hold of the tongs in his two hands, and as he told the story he would stir them about through the ashes.

Says he, "I want to tell you that my father afore he died was a very rich man and owned no end of land. He had three sons, myself and Teddy and Tom ; and the three of us were three good, hard workers. I always liked Teddy and Tom ; but however it came out, Tom and Teddy hated me, and they never lost a chance of trying to damage me with my father and turn him against me. He sent Teddy and Tom to school and gave them a grand education, but he only gave me the spade in my fist and sent me out to the fields. And when Teddy and Tom came back from school, they were two gentlemen, and use to ride their horses and hunt with their hounds ; and me they always made look after the horses and groom them and saddle them and

Manis the Miller

bridle them, and be there in the yard to meet them when they would come in from their riding, and take charge of their horses, give them a rubbing down, and stable them for them.

"In my own mind, I use to think that this wasn't exactly fair or brotherly treatment : but I said nothing, for I liked both Teddy and Tom. And prouder and prouder of them every day got my father, and more and more every day he disliked me, until at long and at last, when he came to die, he liked Teddy and Tom that much, and he liked poor Manis that little, that he drew up his will and divided his land into four parts and left it in this way :

"Now, supposin'," says Manis, says he, digging the point of the tongs into the scowder, "supposin'," says he, "there was my father's farm. He cut it across this way," says he, drawing the tongs through the scowder in one way. "Then he cut it across this way," says he, drawing the tongs through the scowder in the other direction ; "and that quarter," says he, tossing away a quarter of the scowder with the point of the tongs, "he gave to my mother. And that quarter there," says he, tossing off the other quarter into the dirt, "he gave to Teddy, and this quarter here," says he, tossing the third quarter, "he gave to Tom. And this last quarter," says Manis, says he, digging the point of the tongs right into the heart of the other quarter of the scowder, and lifting it up and looking at it, "this quarter," says he, "he gave to the priest," and he pitched it as far from him down the floor as he could. "And there," says he, throwing down the tongs, "he left poor Manis what he is to-day—a beggar and an outcast! That, ma'am," says he, "is my story, and now that I've relieved my mind, I'll sleep sound and well till morning." And down he stretched himself by the fireside, and begins to snore again.

And the old woman she started up to the room, and she told the old man what had happened to the scowder; and the old fellow got into a mighty rage entirely, and was for getting up and going down to have the life of Manis, for he was starving with the hunger. But she tried to soothe him as well as she could. And then he told her to go down to the kitchen and make something else on the fire for him.

"O, it's no use," says she, "a-trying to make anything on the fire, for there'll be some other ache coming on that fellow's ankle or some other trouble on his mind, and he'll be getting up in the middle of it all to tell me about it. But I'll

She reached it to him in
the dark.

Manis the Miller

tell you what I'll do," says she, "I'll go out and I'll milk the cow, and give you a good jug of sweet milk to drink, and that will take the hunger off you till morning."

He told her to get up quick and do it, or she would find him dead of the hunger.

And off she went as quickly as she could, and took a jug off the kitchen dresser, and slipped out, leaving Manis snoring loudly in the kitchen. But when Manis thought that she had had time to have the jug near filled from the cow, he slips out to the byre, and as it was dark he talked like the old man : "And," says he, "I'll die with the hunger if you don't hurry with that."

So she filled the jug, and she reached it to him in the dark, and he drank it off, and gave her back the empty jug, and went in and lay down.

Then she milked off another jug for herself and drank it, and came slipping in, and put the jug easy on the dresser, so as not to waken Manis, and went up to the room.

When she came up, the old fellow was raging there. Says he : "You might have milked all the cows in the county since, an' me dead with hunger here waitin' on it. Give me my jug of milk," says he.

"And what do ye mean?" says she.

Donegal Fairy Stories

"What does yourself mean, you old blather-skite?" says the old man, says he.

Says she, "Didn't you come out to the byre and ask me for the jug of milk there, an' didn't I give it to you, and didn't you drink it all?"

"Be this and be that," says he, "but this is a nice how-do-ye-do. It's that scoundrel," says he, "in the kitchen that's tricked ye again. An' be this an' be that," says he, "I'm goin' down now to have his life."

And when she heard how she had been tricked, she was not a bit sorry to let him go and have Manis's life.

But Manis had been listening with his ear to the keyhole to hear what was going on, and when he heard this, and while the man was preparing to go down and take his life, he hauled in a calf, and put it by the fireside where he had been lying, and threw the cover over it.

And when the man came down with the sledge-hammer, he went to the place where he knew Manis had been lying, and he struck with all his might, and he drove the hammer through the calf's skull, and the calf only just gave one *moo!* and died. And then the old fellow went back to his bed content, and the miller went out and off home again.

He hauled in a calf.

Manis the Miller

When the old fellow and his woman got up in the morning early to go and bury the miller, they found the trick he had played on them, and they were in a pretty rage. But when the breakfast was made this morning, and Donal and all of them sat down, I can tell you the old fellow was in no hurry saying grace, and Donal he got his hearty fill for once in his life anyhow, and so did he at night.

And when Donal was going back home on Monday morning, he leapt the mill-race, and Manis came out, and gave him a cheer. He took Manis's both hands, and he shook them right hearty.

And every Monday morning after, for the three years that the old fellow lived, Manis always saw Donal leap the mill-race as easy as a sparrow might hop over a rod.

At the end of the three years, the old fellow died, and Donal went to live on the farm altogether, and there was no friend ever came to see him that was more heartily welcomed than Manis the Miller.

Hookedy-Crookedy

Ḣookedy-Crookedy

ONCE on a time there was a King and Queen in Ireland, and they had one son named Jack, and when Jack grew up to be man big, he rose up one day and said to his father and mother that he would go off and push his fortune.

All his father and mother could say to Jack, they could not keep him from going. So with his staff in his hand and his father's and mother's blessing on his head, off he started, and he traveled away far, farther than I could tell you, and twice as far as you could tell me. At length one day, coming up to a big wood, he met a gray-haired old man. The old man asked him, "Jack, where are you going?"

He says, "I am going to push my fortune."

Donegal Fairy Stories

"Well," says the old man, says he, "if 'tis looking for service you are, there is a Giant who lives at the other side of that wood that they call the Giant of the Hundred Hills, and I believe he wants a fine, strong, able, clever young fellow like you."

"Very well," says Jack, "I will push on to him."

Push on Jack did, away through the wood, until he got to the other side, and then he saw a big castle, and going up he knocked at the door, and a big Giant came out.

"Welcome, Jack," says he, "the King of Ireland's Son! Where are you going and what do you want?"

"I come," says Jack, "to push my fortune, and am looking for honest service. I have been told," he says to the Giant of the Hundred Hills, "that you wanted a clean, clever boy like me."

"Well," says the Giant, "I am the Giant of the Hundred Hills, and do want such a fine fellow as you. I have to go away every day," he says, "to battle with another giant at the other end of the world, and when I am away, I want somebody to look after my house and place. If you will be of good, faithful service to me, and

Ꞡookedy-Crookedy

do everything I tell you, I will give you a bag of gold at the end of the time."

Jack promised he would do all that. The Giant then gave him a hearty supper and a good bed, and well he slept that night. In the morning the Giant had him called up before the first lark was in the sky.

"Jack, my brave boy," says he, "I have got to be off to the other end of the world to-day to fight the Giant of the Four Winds, and it is time you were up and looking after your business. You have got to put this house in order, and look after everything in it until I come back to-night. To every room in the house and to every place about the house you can go, except the stable. My stable door is closed, and on the peril of your life, don't open it or go into the stable. Keep that in mind."

Jack said he certainly would. Then the Giant visited the stable, and started off; and as soon as he was gone, Jack went fixing and arranging the house and setting everything in order. And a wonderful house it was to Jack, so big and so great; and after that he went to the castle yard and into every house and building there, except the stable: and when he had visited all the rest of them, he stood before the stable and looked at it a long time. "And I wonder," says Jack, says he, "I wonder what can be in there, and what is the reason he wants me on the peril of my life not to go into it? I would like to go and peep in, and there certainly would be no harm."

Every door in and about the Giant's place was opened by a little ring turning on a pivot in the middle of the door. Forward to the stable door Jack then steps, turns the little ring, and the door flew open. Inside what does Jack see but a mare and a bear standing by the manger, and neither of them eating. There was hay before the bear and meat before the mare.

"Well," says Jack, "it is no wonder, poor creatures, you are not eatin'. That was a nice blunder of the Giant," and he stepped in and changed their food, putting hay before the mare and meat before the bear, and at once both of them fell to it and Jack went out and closed the stable door. As he did so his finger stuck in the ring, and he pulled and struggled to get it away, but he could not.

That was a fix for poor Jack, "And by this and by that," says he, "the Giant will be back and find me stuck here;" so he whips out his knife, and cuts off his finger, and leaves it there.

Ḣookedy-Crookedy

And when the Giant came home that night, says he to Jack, "Well, Jack, what sort of a day have you had this day, and how did you get along?"

"I had a fine day," says Jack, "and got along very well indeed."

"Jack," says he, "show me your two hands;" and when Jack held out his two hands, the Giant saw one of his fingers gone. He got black in the face with rage when he saw this, and he said, "Jack, did I not warn you on the peril of your life not to go into that stable?"

Poor Jack pleaded all he could, and said he did not mean to, but curiosity got the best of him, and he thought he would open the door and peep in.

Says the Giant, "No man before ever opened that stable door and lived to tell it, and you, too, would be a dead man this minute only for one thing. Your father's father did my father a great service once. I am the man who never forgets a good thing, and for that service," says he, "I give you your life and pardon this time ; but if you ever do the like again, you won't live."

Jack, he promised that surely and surely he would never do the like again. His supper he got that night, and to bed. And at early morning again the Giant had him up, and, "Jack," says he, "I must be off to the other end of the world again and fight the Giant of the Four Winds. You know your duty is—look after this house and place and set everything in order about it, and go everywhere you like, only don't open the stable door or go into the stable, on the peril of your life."

"I will mind all that," says Jack.

Then that morning again the Giant visited the stable before he went away. And after the Giant had gone, to his work went Jack, wandering through the house, cleaning and setting everything in order about it, and out into the yard he went, and fixed and arranged everything out there, except the stable. He stood before the stable door a good while this day, and says he to himself, " I wonder how the bear and the mare are doing, and what the Giant did when he went in to see them? I would give a great deal to know," says he. " I will take a peep in."

Into the ring of the door he put his finger, and turned it, and looked in, and there he saw the mare and the bear standing as no the day before and neither of them eating. In Jack steps. "And no wonder, poor creatures," says he, "you don't eat, when that is the way the Giant blundered,"

Dookedy-Crookedy

he says, after he saw the meat before the mare and the hay before the bear this time also.

Jack then changed the food, putting the hay before the mare and the meat before the bear, as it should be, and very soon both the mare and the bear were eating heartily ; and then Jack went out. He closed the door, and when he did so, his finger stuck in the ring; and pull and struggle though Jack did, he could not get it out.

"Och, och, och," says Jack, says he, "I am a dead man to-day surely."

He whips out his knife, and cuts off his finger, and leaves it there, and 'twas there when the Giant came home that night.

" Well, Jack, my fine boy," says he, " how have you got on to-day ? "

"Oh, finely, finely," says Jack, says he, holding his hands behind his back all the same.

" Show me your hands, Jack," says the Giant, " till I see if you wash them and keep them clean always." And when Jack showed his hands, the Giant got black in the face with rage, and says he. " Didn't I forgive you your life yesterday for going into that stable, and you promised never to do it again, and here I find you out, once more ? "

The Giant ranted and raged for a long time,

and then says he, " Because your father's father did my father such a good turn, I suppose I will have to spare your life this second time ; but, Jack," says he, "if you should live for a hundred years, and spend them all in my service, and if you should then again open that door and put your foot into my stable, that day," says he, " you will be a dead man as sure as there is a head on you. Mind that !"

Jack, he thanked the Giant very much for sparing his life, and promised that he never, never would again disobey him.

The next morning the Giant had Jack up early, and told him he was going off this day to fight the Giant at the other end of the world, and gave Jack his directions, and warned him just as on the other days. Then he went into the stable before he went away. And when he was gone, Jack went through all the house, and through the whole yard, setting everything in order, and when everything was done, he stood before the stable door.

"I wonder," says Jack, " how the poor mare and the poor bear are getting along and what the Giant of the Hundred Hills was doing here to-day? I should very much like," says he, "to take one wee, wee peep in," and he opened the door.

Ђookedy-Crookedy

Jack peeped in, and there the mare and the bear stood looking at each other again, and neither of them taking a morsel. And there was the meat before the mare and the hay before the bear, just as on the other days.

"Poor creatures," says Jack, "it is no wonder you are not eating, and hungry and hungry you must be." And forward he steps, and changes the food, putting it as it should be, the hay before the mare and the meat before the bear, and to it both of them fell.

And when he had done this, up speaks the mare, and "Poor Jack," says she, "I am sorry for you. This night you will be killed surely; and sorry for us, too, I am, for we will be killed as well as you."

"Oh, Oh, Oh!" says Jack, says he, "that is terrible. Is there nothing we can do ?"

"Only one thing," says the mare.

"What is that ?" says Jack.

"It's this," says the mare; "put that saddle and bridle on me, and let us start off and be away, far, far from this country, when the Giant comes back." And soon Jack had the saddle and bridle on the mare, and on her back he got to start off.

"Oh!" says the bear, speaking up, "both of

you are going away to leave me in for all the trouble."

"No," says the mare, "we will not do that. Jack," says she, "take the chains and tie me to the bear."

Jack tied the mare to the bear with chains that were hanging by, and then the three of them, the mare and the bear and Jack, started, and on and on they went, as fast as they could gallop.

After a long time, says the mare: "Jack, look behind you, and see what you can see."

Jack looked behind him, and "Oh!" says he, "I see the Giant of the Hundred Hills coming like a raging storm. Very soon he will be on us, and we will all three be murdered."

Says the mare, says she, "We have a chance yet. Look in my left ear, and see what you can see;" and in her left ear Jack looked, and saw a little chestnut.

"Throw it over your left shoulder," says the mare.

Jack threw it over his left shoulder, and that minute there arose behind them a chestnut wood ten miles wide. On and on they went that day and that night; and till middle of the next day, "Jack," says the mare, "look behind you, and see what you can see."

Hookedy-Crookedy

Jack looked behind him, and "Oh!" says he, "I see the Giant of the Hundred Hills coming tearing after us like a harvest hurricane."

"Do you see anything strange about him, Jack?" says the mare.

"Yes," says Jack, says he, "there are as many bushes on the top of his head, and as much fowl stuck about his feet and legs as will keep him in fire-wood and flesh for years to come. We are done for this time, entirely," says poor Jack.

"Not yet," says the mare; "there is another chance. Look into my right ear, and see what you can see."

In the mare's right ear Jack looked, and found a drop of water.

"Throw it over your left shoulder, Jack," says the mare, "and see what will happen."

Over his left shoulder Jack threw it, and all at once a lough sprung up between them and the Giant that was one hundred miles wide every way and one hundred miles deep.

"Now," says the mare, "he cannot reach us until he drinks his way through the lough, and very likely he will drink until he bursts, and then we shall be rid of him altogether."

Jack thanked God, and on he went. It was not

Donegal Fairy Stories

long now until he reached the borders of Scotland, and there he saw a great wood.

"Now," says the mare and the bear, "this wood must be our hiding-place."

"And what about me?" says Jack.

"For you, Jack," says the mare, "you must push on and look for employment. The castle of the King of Scotland is near by, and I think you will be likely to get employment there; but first I must change you into an ugly little hookedy-crookedy fellow, because the King of Scotland has three beautiful daughters, and he won't take into his service a handsome fellow as you, for fear his daughters would fall in love with you."

Then the mare put her nostrils to Jack's breast and blew her breath over him, and Jack was turned into an ugly little hookedy-crookedy fellow.

"Jack," says the mare, "before you go, look into my left ear, and take what you see there."

Out of the mare's left ear Jack took a little cap.

"Jack," says she, "that is a wishing-cap, and every time you put it on and wish to have anything done, it will be done. Whenever you are in any trouble," the mare says, "come back to me, and I will do what I can for you, and now good-bye."

The mare blew her breath over him and Jack was turned into an ugly little hookedy-crookedy fellow.

Hookedy-Crookedy

So Jack said good-bye to the mare and to the bear, and set off. When he got out of the wood, he soon saw a castle, and walked up to it and went in by the kitchen. A servant was employed scouring knives. He told her he wanted employment. She said the King of Scotland would employ no man in his house, so he might as well push on. But Jack insisted that the King would employ him, and at length the girl consented to go and let the King know.

When the girl had gone away, Jack put on his wishing-cap and wished the knives and forks scoured, and all at once the knives and forks, that were piled in a stack ten yards high, were scoured as brightly as new pins ; and though the King of Scotland did not want to employ him, when he found how quickly Jack had scoured all the big stack of knives and forks, he agreed to keep him. But first he brought down his three daughters to see Jack, so that he could observe what impression Jack made upon them. When they came into the kitchen and saw the ugly little fellow, every one of the three fainted and had to be carried out.

" It is all right," says the King; "we will surely keep you," and Jack was employed, and sent out into the garden to work there.

Donegal fairy Stories

Now at this time the King of the East declared war on the King of Scotland. The King of the East had a mighty army entirely, and he threatened to wipe the King of Scotland off the face of the earth.

The King of Scotland was very much troubled, and he consulted with his Grand Adviser what was best to be done, and his Grand Adviser counseled that he should at once give his three daughters in marriage to sons of kings, and in that way get great help for the war. The King said this was a grand idea.

So he sent out messengers to all parts of the world to say that his three beautiful daughters were open for marriage. In a very short time the son of the King of Spain came and married the eldest daughter, and the son of the King of France came and married the second, and a whole lot of princes came looking for the youngest, who was the most beautiful of the three and whose name was Yellow Rose ; but she would not take one of them, and for this the King ordered her never to come into his sight, nor into company, again.

Yellow Rose got very downhearted, and spent almost all her time now wandering in the garden, where the Hookedy-Crookedy was looking

Ďookedy-Crookedy

after the flowers, and she used to come around again and again, chatting to Hookedy-Crookedy. And so it was not long until Hookedy-Crookedy saw that the Yellow Rose was in love with him, and he got just as deeply in love with her, for she was a beautiful and charming girl.

The next thing the Grand Adviser counseled the King was that he should send his two new sons-in-law, the Prince of Spain and the Prince of France, to the Well of the World's End for bottles of loca* to take to battle with them, that they might cure the wounded and dead men. So the King ordered his sons-in-law to go to the Well of the World's End and bring him back two bottles of loca.

The Yellow Rose told Hookedy-Crookedy all about this, and when he had turned it over in his mind, he said to himself, "I will go and have a chat with the mare and the bear about this."

So off to the woods he went, and right glad the mare and the bear were to see him. He told them all that had happened, and then he told them how the King's two sons-in-law were to start to the Well of the World's End the next day, and asked the mare's advice about it.

"Well, Jack," says the mare, "I want you to

---

* loca was a liquid that cured all wounds and restored the dead to life.

go with them. Take an old hunter in the King's stable, an old bony, skinny animal that is past all work, and put an old straw saddle on him, and dress yourself in the most ragged dress you can get, and join the two men on the road, and say that you are going with them. They will be heartily ashamed of you, Jack, and your old horse, and they will do everything to get rid of you. When you come to the cross-roads, one of them will propose to go in and have a drink; and while you are chatting over your drink, they will propose that the three of you separate and every one take a road by himself to go to the Well of the World's End, and that all three shall meet at the cross-roads again, and whoever is back first with the bottle of water is to be the greatest hero of them all. You agree to this. When they start on their roads, they will not go many miles till they fill their bottles from spring wells by the roadside and hurry back to the meeting-place, and then continue on home to the King of Scotland and give him these bottles as bottles of Ioca from the Well of the World's End. But you will be before them. After you have set out on the road, and when you have gone around the first bend, put on your wishing-cap and wish for two bottles of Ioca from the Well of the

Ʀookedy-Crookedy

World's End, and at once you will have them."
And then the mare directed Jack fully all that he
was to do after.

Jack thanked the mare, and bade goodby to
her, and went away.

The next day, when the King's two sons-in-
law set out on their grand steeds to go to the Well
of the World's End, they had not gone far when
Jack, in a ragged old suit and sitting on a straw
saddle on an old white skinny horse, joined them
and told them he too was going with them for a
bottle of Ioca. Right heartily ashamed were
they of Jack and ready to do anything to get rid
of him.

By and by, when they came to where the road
divided into three, they proposed to have a drink,
and as they set off to drink they proposed that
each take a road for himself, and whoever got
back first with a bottle of Ioca would be the
greatest hero. All agreed, and each chose his
own road and set out.

When Jack had got around the first bend, he
put on his wishing-cap and wished for two bottles of Ioca from the Well of the World's End,
and no sooner had he wished than he had them;
and back again he came, and when the other two
came riding up, surprised they were to find Jack

there before them. They said that Jack had not been to the Well of the World's End and it was no Ioca he had with him, but some water from the roadside.

Said Jack, "Take care that is not your own story. Just test them; when the servant comes in, you cut off his head and then cure him with water from your bottles."

But both refused to do this, for they knew the water in their bottles could not cure anything, and they defied Jack to do it.

"Very soon I will do it," said Jack.

So when the servant came in with the bottles of Ioca, Jack drew his sword and whipped his head off him, and in a minute's time, with two drops from one of his bottles, he had the head on again.

Says they to Hookedy-Crookedy, "What will you take for your two bottles?"

Says Jack, "I will take the golden balls of your marriage pledge, and also you shall allow me to write something on your backs."

And they agreed to this. They handed over to Jack the two golden balls that were their marriage tokens, and they let Jack write on their bare backs; and what Jack wrote on each of them was, "This is an unlawfully married man." Then he gave them the bottles of Ioca, and they

Hookedy-Crookedy

brought them to the King, and Jack returned to his garden again.

He did not tell the Yellow Rose where he had been and what doing, only said he was away on a message for her father. As soon as the King got the bottles of loca, he gave orders that his army should move to battle the next day.

The next morning early Jack was over to the wood to consult the mare. He told her what was going to happen that day. Says the mare, "Look in my left ear, Jack, and see what you will see."

Jack looked in the mare's left ear, and took out of it a grand soldier's dress. The mare told him to put it on and get on her back. On he put the dress, and at once Hookedy-Crookedy was transformed into a very handsome, dashing young fellow, and off went Jack and the mare and the bear, the three of them, away to the war. Every one saw them, and they admired Jack very much, he was such a handsome, clever-looking fellow, and word was passed on to the King about the great Prince who was riding to the war—himself, the mare, and the bear. The King came to see him, too, and asked him on which side he was going to fight.

" I will strike no stroke this day," says Jack, " except on the side of the King of Scotland."

Donegal Fairy Stories

The King thanked him very heartily, and said he was sure they would win. So they went into the battle with Jack at their head, and Jack struck east and west and in all directions, and at every blow of his sword the wind of his stroke tossed houses on the other side of the world, and in a very short time the King of the East ran off, with all his army that were still left alive. Then the King of Scotland invited Jack to come home with him, as he was going to give a great feast in his honor ; but Jack said no, he could not go.

"They don't know at home," said Jack, "where I am at all"—and neither they did—"so I must be off to them as quickly as possible."

"Then," says the King, "the least I can do is to give you a present. Here is a table-cloth," says he, "and every time you spread it out you will have it covered with eating and drinking of all sorts."

Jack took it, and thanked him, and rode away. He left the mare and the bear in their own wood, and became Hookedy-Crookedy again, and ran back to his garden. The Yellow Rose told him of the brave soldier that had won her father's battle that day.

"Well, well," says Jack, says he, "he must

Hookedy-Crookedy

have been a grand fellow entirely. It is a pity I was not there, but I had to go on a message for the King."

"Poor Hookedy-Crookedy," says she, "what could you do if you were there yourself?"

Jack went to the wood again next morning, and consulted with the mare.

"Jack," said the mare, "look in the inside of my left ear, and see what you will see," and Jack took out of her left ear a soldier's suit, done off with silver, the grandest ever seen, and at the mare's advice he put the suit on, and mounted on her back, and the three of them went off to the battle. Every one was admiring the beautiful, dashing fellow that was riding to the battle this day, and word came to the King, and the King came to speak to him and welcomed him heartily.

He said, "Your brother came with us the last day we went into the battle. Your brother is a very handsome, fine-looking fellow. What side are you going to fight on?"

Says Jack, "I will strike no stroke on any side but yours this day."

The King thanked him very heartily, and into the battle they went with Jack at their head, and Jack struck east and west and in all directions,

Donegal Fairy Stories

and the wind of the strokes blew down forests in the other end of the world, and very soon the King of the East, with all his army that were still alive, drew off from the battle.

Then the King thanked Jack and invited him to his castle, where he would give a feast in his honor. But Jack said he could not go, for they did not know at home where he was, and they would be uneasy about him until he reached home again.

"Then," says the King, "the least I can do for you is to give you a present. Here is a purse, and no matter how often and how much you pay out of it, it will never be empty."

Jack took it, and thanked him, and rode away. In the wood he left the mare and the bear, and was again changed into Hookedy-Crookedy, and went home to his garden. The Yellow Rose came out, and told him about the great victory a brave and beautiful soldier, brother to the fine fellow of the day before, had won for her father.

"Well, well," says Jack, says he, "that was very wonderful entirely. I am sorry I was not there, but I had to be away on a message for your father."

"But, my poor Hookedy-Crookedy," says she, "it was better so, for what could you do?"

Hookedy-Crookedy

Three days after that the King of the East took courage to come to battle again. The morning of the battle Jack went to the wood to consult the mare.

"Look into my left ear, Jack, and see what you will see," and from the mare's left ear Jack drew out a most gorgeous soldier's suit, done off with gold braiding and ornaments of every sort. By the mare's advice he put it on, and himself, the mare, and the bear went off to the war.

The King soon heard of the wonderfully grand fellow that was riding to the war to-day with the mare and the bear, and he came to Jack and welcomed him and told him how his two brothers had won the last two victories for him. He asked Jack on what side he was going to fight.

"I will strike no stroke this day," says Jack, "only on the King of Scotland's side."

The King thanked him heartily, and said, "We will surely win the victory," and then into the battle they rode with Jack at their head, and Jack struck east and west and in all directions, and the wind of the strokes tumbled mountains at the other end of the world, and very soon the King of the East with all his army that were left alive took to their heels and never stopped running until they went as far as the world would let them.

Then the King came to Jack and thanked him over and over again, and said he would never be able to repay him. He then invited him to come to his castle, where he would give a little feast in his honor, but Jack said they didn't know at home where he was and they would be uneasy about him, and so he could not go with the King.

"But," says he, "I and my brothers will come to feast with you at any other time."

"What day will the three of you come?" said the King.

"Only one of us can leave home in one day," said Jack. "I will come to feast with you to-morrow, and my second brother the day after, and my third brother the day after that."

The King agreed to this and thanked him. "And now," said the King, "let me give you a present," and he gave him a comb, such that every time he combed his hair with it he would comb out of it bushels of gold and silver, and it would transform the ugliest man that ever was into the nicest and handsomest. Jack took it and thanked the King and rode away.

Hookedy-Crookedy

On this day, as on the other two days after the battle, they cured the dead and the wounded with the bottles of loca, and all were well again. When Jack went to the wood, he left the mare and the bear in it and became Hookedy-Crookedy again, and went home and to his garden. The Yellow Rose came to him and had wonderful news for him this day about the terrible grand fellow entirely, who had won the battle for her father that day ; brother to the two brave fellows who had won the battles on the other two days.

"Well," says Jack, says he, "those must be wonderful chaps. I wish I had been there; but I had to be away on a message for your father all day."

"Oh, my poor Hookedy-Crookedy," says she, "it was better so, for what could you do ?"

The next day, when it was near dinner time, he went off to the wood to the mare and the bear and got on the suit he had worn the day before in the battle, and mounted the mare and rode for the castle, and when he came there all the gates happened to be closed, but he put the mare at the walls, which were nine miles high, and leapt them.

The King scolded the gate-keepers, but Jack

said a trifle like that didn't harm him or his mare. After dinner the King asked him what he thought of his two daughters and their husbands. Jack said they were very good and asked him if he had any more daughters in his family.

The King said he used to have another, the youngest, but she would not consent to marry as he wished, and he had banished her out of his sight.

Jack said he would like to see her.

The King said he never wished to let her enter company again, but he could not refuse Jack; so the Yellow Rose was sent for.

Jack fell a-chatting with her and used all his arts to win her, and of course, in this handsome Jack she did not recognize ugly little Hookedy-Crookedy. He told her he had heard that she had the very bad taste to fall in love with an ugly, crooked, wee fellow in her father's garden.

"I am a handsome fellow, and a rich prince," says Jack, "and I will give you myself and all I possess if you will only say you will accept me."

She was highly insulted, and she showed him that very quickly. She said, "I won't sit here and hear the man I love abused;" and she got up to leave.

"Well," says Jack, "I admire your spirit;

Ꮲookedy-Crookedy

but before you go," says he, "let me make you a little present," and he handed her a tablecloth. "There," says he, "if you marry Hookedy-Crookedy, as long as you have this tablecloth, you will never want eating and drinking of the best."

The other two sisters grabbed to get the tablecloth from her, but Jack put out his hands and pushed them back.

At dinner-time the next day Jack came in the dress in which he had gone into the second battle, and with the mare he cleared the walls as on the day before.

The King was enraged at the gate-keepers and began to scold them, but Jack laughed at them and said a trifle like that was nothing to him or his mare.

After dinner was over the King asked what he thought of his two daughters and their husbands.

Jack said they were very good, and asked him if he had any more daughters in his family.

The King said, "I have no more except one who won't do as I wish and who has fallen in love with an ugly, crooked, wee fellow in my garden, and I ordered her never to come into my sight."

But Jack said he would very much like to see her.

Donegal fairy Stories

The King said that on Jack's account he would break his vow and let her come in. So the Yellow Rose was brought in, and Jack fell to chatting with her. He did all he could to make her fall in love with him, and told her of all his great wealth and possessions and offered himself to her, and said if she only would marry him she should live in ease and luxury and happiness all the days of her life, as she never could do with Hookedy-Crookedy.

But Yellow Rose got very angry, and said: " I won't sit here and listen to such things," and she got up to leave the room.

" Well," says Jack, " I admire your spirit, and before you go let me make you a little present."

So he handed her a purse. " Here," says he, " is a purse, and all the days yourself and Hookedy-Crookedy live you will never want for money, for that purse will never be empty.

Her sisters made a grab to snatch it from her, but Jack shoved them back, and went out. And Jack rode away with the mare after dinner and left her in the wood.

When he came back to his garden he always came in the Hookedy-Crookedy shape and always pretended he had been off on a message for the King.

Ḥookedy-Crookedy

The third day he went to the wood again. He dressed in the suit in which he had gone to the first battle, and when he came back he went to the castle and cleared the walls, and when the King scolded the gate-keepers Jack told him never to mind, as that was a small trifle to him and his mare.

A very grand dinner indeed Jack had this day, and when they chatted after dinner the King asked him how he liked his two daughters and their husbands.

He said he liked them very well, and asked him if he had any more daughters in his family.

The King said no, except one foolish one who wouldn't do as he wished, and who had fallen in love with an ugly, crooked, wee fellow in his garden, and she was never to come within his sight again.

Says Jack, '' I would like to see that girl.''

The King said he could not refuse Jack any request he made, so he sent for the Yellow Rose. When she came in, Jack fell into chat with her, and did his very, very best to make her fall in love with him. But it was of no use. He told her of all his wealth and all his grand possessions, and said if she would marry him she should own all these, and all the days she should live she

Donegal Fairy Stories

should be the happiest woman in the wide world, but if she married Hookedy-Crookedy, he said, she would never be free from want and hardships, besides having an ugly husband.

If the Yellow Rose was in a rage on the two days before, she was in a far greater rage now. She said she wouldn't sit there to listen. She told Jack that Hookedy-Crookedy was in her eyes a far more handsome and beautiful man than he or than any king's son she had ever seen. She said to Jack, that if he were ten times as handsome and a hundred times as wealthy, she wouldn't give Hookedy-Crookedy's little finger for himself, or for all his wealth and possessions, and then she got up to leave the room.

" Well," says Jack, says he, " I admire your spirit very much, and," says he, " I would like to make you a little present. Here is a comb," he said, " and it will comb out of your hair a bushel of gold and a bushel of silver every time you comb with it, and, besides," says he, "it will make handsome the ugliest man that ever was."

When the other sisters heard this they rushed to snatch the comb from her, but Jack threw them backwards so very roughly that their husbands sprang at him. With a back switch of his

Hookedy-Crookedy

two hands Jack knocked the husbands down senseless The King flew into a rage, and said, "How dare you do that to the two finest and bravest men of this world?"

"Fine and brave, indeed!" said Jack. "One and the other they are worthless creatures, and not even your lawful sons-in-law."

" How dare you say that?" says the King.

"Strip their backs where they lie and see for yourself." And there the King saw written, "An unlawfully married man."

"What is the meaning of this?" says the King. "They were lawfully married to my two daughters, and they have the golden tokens of the marriage."

Jack drew out from his pocket the golden balls and handed them to the King, and said, "It is I who have the tokens."

The Yellow Rose had gone off to the garden in the middle of all this. Jack made the King sit down, and told him all his story, and how he came by the golden balls. He told him how he was Hookedy-Crookedy, and that it reflected a great deal of honor on his youngest daughter that she whom the King thought so worthless should refuse to give up Hookedy-Crookedy for the one she thought a wealthy prince. The King, you may be sure, was now highly delighted to grant him all he desired. A couple of drops of Ioca brought the King's two sons to their senses again, and at Jack's request, they were ordered to go and live elsewhere. Jack went off, left his mare in the wood, and came into the garden as Hookedy-Crookedy. He told the Yellow Rose he had been gathering bilberries.

"Oh," says she, "I have something grand for you. Let me comb your hair with this comb."

Hookedy-Crookedy put his head in her lap, and she combed out a bushel of gold and silver ; and when he stood up again, she saw Hookedy-Crookedy no more, but instead the beautiful prince that had been trying to win her in her father's drawing-room for the last three days; and then and there to her Jack told his whole story, and it's Yellow Rose who is the delighted girl.

With little delay they were married. The wedding lasted a year and a day, and there were five hundred fiddlers, five hundred fluters and a thousand fifers at it, and the last day was better than the first.

Shortly after the marriage, Jack and his bride were out walking one day. A beautiful young woman crossed their path. Jack addressed her, but she gave him a very curt reply.

Hookedy-Crookedy put his
head in her lap, and she
combed out a bushel of
gold and silver.

Hookedy-Crookedy

"Your manners are not so handsome as your looks," said Jack to her.

"And bad as they are, they are better than your memory, Hookedy-Crookedy," says she.

"What do you mean?" says Jack.

She led Jack aside, and she told him, "I am the mare who was so good to you. I was condemned to that shape for a number of years, and now my enchantment is over. I had a brother who was enchanted into a bear, and whose enchantment is over now also. I had hopes," she says, "that some day you would be my husband, but I see," she says, "that you quickly forgot all about me. No matter now," she says; "I couldn't wish you a better and handsomer wife than you have got. Go home to your castle, and be happy and live prosperous. I shall never see you, and you will never see me again."

Donal That Was Rich and Jack That Was Poor

Donal That Was Rich and Jack That Was Poor

NCE there were two brothers named Donal and Jack. Donal was hired by a rich man who had one daughter, and when his master died, he married the daughter.

Jack, he lived close by, with his wife and a big family of children, and he was very poor; but Donal, he was no way good to Jack, and would never reach his hand to him with a thing. And when the hunger would come into Jack's house, Jack, he used to think it little harm to steal a bullock out of Donal's big flock, and kill it for his family.

At length Donal began to suspect that Jack was taking his bullocks, but he didn't know how he would find out for sure. Donal's old mother-in-law proposed a plan by which she could catch Jack.   She made Donal put her into a big chest that had little spy-holes in it, and put in with her beef and brandy enough to last her nine days.   Then Donal was to take the chest to Jack's, and have it left there on some excuse.

Donal went to Jack, and said he had a big chest of things that was in his way, and asked Jack if he would be so good as to allow him to leave it in his kitchen for a week or so.   Jack said he was very welcome to put in ten chests if he liked.   So Donal had the chest with the mother-in-law and her provisions in it, carried to Jack's, and planted in a good place in the kitchen.

On the very first night that the chest and the mother-in-law were at Jack's, he stole and killed and brought in another bullock, and the old woman was watching it all through the spy-holes of the chest.   And after Jack and his wife and children had eaten a hearty supper off the bullock, he and his wife began talking over one thing and another, and says he: "I'd like to know what Donal has in that chest."

So off he went to a locksmith, and he got the loan of a whole bundle of keys, and he came and tried them all in the chest till he got one that opened it.

When Donal found what was in the chest, he

Jack took the old woman's
body on his shoulder and
carried her off to Donal.

Donal Rich and Jack Poor

lost little time taking away the beef and the brandy, and he put in their place empty bottles and clean-picked bones, and locked the old woman up with these again.

At the end of nine days, Donal came for the chest. He thanked Jack for giving him house room for it for so long, and said he had now room for it himself and so he had come to take it home. And behold you, when Donal and his wife opened the chest at home, there was the old woman dead of starvation, and a lot of bones and empty bottles in the chest.

Says Donal: "She got greedy, and ate and drank the whole of the provisions the first day, and this is her deserving."

Well, Donal and the wife waked her and buried her, with a purse of money under her head to pay her way in the next world, as they used to do in those days.

Jack, of course, he went to the wake and to the funeral, and sympathized sore with Donal and Donal's wife both. But the very next night after the funeral, Jack dug up the corpse to get the money, as it was so useful to him. Then he took the old woman's body on his shoulder and carried it off to Donal's, and went down into Donal's wine cellar. He put it sitting in a chair by a puncheon there, and put a glass into its hand, and turned on the wine.

In the morning Donal's first race was always to the cellar to have a drink, and when he came down this morning he fell over and fainted with the fright when he saw his old mother-in-law sitting by the puncheon drinking. When he came to himself he had her taken up and laid out in the wake-room again.

Jack, he came walking over to see Donal like to bid him the time of day in the morning. "Good morning to you, Donal," says he, "and how do you find yourself this morning?"

"Och! Och! Och! Jack! Jack!" says Donal, says he, "I'm in a terrible fix entirely."

"Why, what's the matter?" says Jack.

"Why," says he, "my old mother-in-law got up out of the grave in the night time and came back; and when I went down to the cellar in the morning to get a drink of wine, there was the old lady sitting by the puncheon, and she having the puncheon drunk empty. What am I to do at all, at all?" says he.

"Well," says Jack, says he, "I know why she got up out of her grave again."

"For what did she?" says Donal.

"Because you didn't bury her half decently,"

He put her sitting in a
chair by a puncheon there.

Donal Rich and Jack Poor

says Jack, "you only put ten pound under her head, and it's fifty pound you should have put."

"Well, I'm sure I'm sorry for that," says Donal, "and I'll make certain that I'll bury her decently enough this time."

So Jack went with him to help him bury her this day again, and he saw Donal put a purse of fifty sovereigns under her head. "Now," says Donal, says he, "she'll surely not come back to bother me."

But that night Jack went to the graveyard and raised the body again, and got the fifty pounds. And he took the body then with him on his shoulder off to Donal's, and he went into the stables, and he put the body sitting on the finest big horse in Donal's stable, and he tied it there, and he tied a sword into its hand. Now Donal was to have gone off next morning, riding on a little black mare that was a favorite of his, to the town to pay the accounts of the funeral; and Jack, he had known this, and when Donal came down in the very early morning, when it was still dark, he went into the stable, and he took out the little black mare.

The horse on which Jack had tied the old woman was a great companion of this little black mare, and both of them used to run on the grass together ; so when the little black mare was taken out by Donal, the horse (which Jack had left loose) trotted out after.

When Donal saw the appearance of the horse coming out of the stable, and on its back the old mother-in-law with the sword lifted up in her hand, he gave a yell, and he jumped up on the mare, and off as fast as he could gallop.

Off after the little mare the big horse started, and the faster Donal went, the faster came the big horse trotting behind him ; and every time he looked over his shoulder, there he saw his old mother-in-law with the sword lifted, ready, as he thought, to cut him down, and all that he could do, he couldn't gain ground.

Jack, he was prepared for all this. He was concealed half a mile along the way, and when Donal came tearing up he came out of where he was concealed, and said to Donal : "What's the matter?"

And Donal pointed back, and Jack he leaped and got hold of the big horse and stopped it, and led it back home, and took the old woman off its back.

When Donal ventured home again, he was in very low spirits entirely, and he said that if his mother-in-law was going to rise every time she

He put the body sitting on the finest big horse in Domal's stable.

Donal Rich and Jack Poor

was buried and haunt him all the days of his life, he might as well end his life at once.

"Not too quick!" says Jack, says he. "What will you give me, and I'll save you from your mother-in-law?"

"O! I'll give you," says he, "anything at all, in moderation, that you ask."

"Well," says Jack, says he, "if you pension me, I'll live here always, and I'll watch by your mother-in-law's grave every night, and keep her from rising."

Says Donal: "If you do that, I'll give you any pension you ask."

Jack asked one hundred pounds a year, and Donal agreed to it. They buried the mother-in-law the third time, and Jack worked for his pension so faithfully and so well, that she never rose more.

Donal and his wife lived middling happy, but Jack and his wife and children, with their pension of one hundred pounds a year, were the happiest family in all Ireland.

The Snow, the Crow, and the Blood

The Snow, the Crow, and the Blood

ONE day in the dead of winter, when the snow lay like a linen tablecloth over the world, Jack, the King of Ireland's son, went out to shoot. He saw a crow, and he shot it, and it fell down on the snow. Jack went up to it, and he thought he never saw anything blacker than that crow, or redder than its blood, nor anything whiter than the snow round about.

He said to himself: "I'll never rest till I get a wife whose hair is as black as that crow, whose cheeks are as red as that blood, and whose skin is as white as that snow."

So he went home, and told his father and mother this. He said he was going to set off before him and look for such a girl.

The King and Queen told Jack that it would

be impossible ever to get a girl that would answer that description, and tried to persuade Jack from setting out, but Jack wouldn't be persuaded.

He started off with his father's and his mother's blessing, and a hundred guineas that his father had given him in his pocket. He traveled away and away very far, and about the middle of the day on the second day out, passing a graveyard, he saw a crowd there wrangling over a corpse. He went in and inquired what was the matter, and he found there were bailiffs wanting to seize the corpse for a debt of a hundred guineas. Jack was sorry for the poor corpse, so he put his hand in his pocket, took out the hundred guineas, and paid them down; and then the friends of the corpse thanked him heartily and buried the body.

That very same evening Jack was overtaken by a little red man who asked him where he was going.

Says Jack: "I'm going in search of a wife."

"Well," says the little red man, "such a handsome young fellow as you won't have to go far."

"Far enough," says Jack, "because the girl I want must have hair as black as the blackest

Jack saw a crow and shot
it and it fell at his feet.

The Snow, Crow, and Blood

crow, cheeks as red as the reddest blood, and skin as white as the whitest snow."

"Then," said the little red man, "there's only one such woman in the world, and she is the Princess of the East. There's many a brave young man went there before you to court her, but none of them ever came back alive again."

"For life or for death," says Jack, "I'll never rest until I reach the Princess of the East and court her."

"Well," said the little red man, "you'll want a boy with you. Let me be your boy."

"But I have no money to pay you," says Jack.

"That will be all right," says the little red man. "I'll go with you."

That night late they reached a great castle. "This castle," says the little red man, "is the castle of the Giant of the Cloak of Darkness."

"Oh," says Jack, "I've heard of that terrible giant. We'll pass on, and look for somewhere else to stop."

"No other place we'll stop than here," says the little red man, knocking at the gates.

Jack was too brave to run away, so he stood by the little red man till a great and terrible giant came to the gates and opened them, and asked them what they wanted.

Donegal Fairy Stories

"We want supper and a bed for the night," says the red fellow.

"That's good," says the giant. "I want supper and bed too. I'll make my supper off you both, and my bed on your bones." And then he let a terrible laugh out of him that made the hair stand up on poor Jack's head.

But in a flash, the wee red fellow whips out his sword and struck out at the giant, and the giant then pulled out his, and struck out at the wee red man. Both of them fell to it hard and fast, and they fought a terrible fight for a long time; but in the end the wee red man ran the giant through the heart and killed him.

Then he took Jack in, and they spread for themselves a grand supper with the best of everything eatable and drinkable, and had a good sleep, and in the morning they started off, the wee red fellow taking with him the Cloak of Darkness belonging to the giant he had killed.

They traveled on and on that day, and at night they reached another castle.

"What castle is this?" says Jack.

"This," says the wee red man, "is the castle of the Giant of the Purse of Plenty."

"Then," says Jack, "I've heard of that terri-

158

The Snow, Crow, and Blood

ble giant. We'll push on and look for somewhere else to stop to-night."

"Nowhere else than here we'll stop," says the
wee red man. "No danger ever frightened me
in all my life before, and it's too late to begin to
learn fright now."

And before Jack could say anything he had
knocked at the gates, and a giant with two heads
came out roaring, and asked them what they
wanted and what brought them there."

"We don't want much," says the little red
man, "only what every traveler expects—a
sweet supper and a soft bed."

"I want both myself, too," says the giant,
"and I'll make a sweet supper off you both, and
a soft bed of your bones."

Then he laughed an awful laugh that shook
the castle and made the hair stand up on poor
Jack's head.

But that minute the wee red man whipped out
his sword and made at him, and the giant
whipped out his and made at the wee red man;
and both of them fell to and had a fight long and
hard, but at length the wee red man ran his
sword through the giant's heart and killed him.

Then they went in, and spread for themselves
a grand supper and a fine bed, in which they

Donegal Fairy Stories

slept soundly till morning. And in the morning they went off, the little red man taking with him the Purse of Plenty.

All that day they traveled on before them, and when night fell they came to another great castle.

"What castle is this?" says Jack.

"This," says the little red man, "is the castle of the Giant of the Sword of Light."

"Oh," says Jack, "I've heard of that terrible giant and his awful sword, and," he says, "I want to get out of his neighborhood as fast as possible."

"Fear never made me turn my back on man or mortal yet," says the little red man, "and I don't think I'll begin this late in life. As we're here, we'll lodge here this night."

So on the gates he rattled, and out came a frightful giant, with three great heads on him, and he roared so that the hills shook; and he asked them what they were doing here and what they wanted.

"We are two poor travelers on a journey," says the little red man, "and as night fell on us we thought we would ask you to give us bed and board for the night."

"Ha! Ha!" says the giant, laughing a terrible

He began whacking and
hacking, hewing and cut-
ting the giant.

The Snow, Crow, and Blood

laugh. " I'll board myself on you two this night, and I'll bed me on your bones."

And at that he drew from his scabbard the terrible Sword of Light, whose flash traveled thrice round the world every time it was drawn, and whose lightest stroke killed any being, natural or enchanted.

But that instant the little red man drew around him the Cloak of Darkness, so that he should disappear from the giant's eyes, and drawing his own sword he began whacking and hacking, hewing and cutting the giant, while the giant couldn't see him to strike him in return, and in two minutes the wee red man had run his sword through the giant's heart and killed him.

He and Jack went into the castle, and they made a hearty supper and slept soundly in the softest beds they could get, and in the morning they went off again, the wee red man taking with him the Sword of Light.

Having the Purse of Plenty, they could not know want from this forward. So they went on their journey right merrily. They traveled far and long until at length they came into the East, and pushed on for the castle of the Princess. And when they came to where the Princess lived, they took their horses (for they were now

163

riding two beautiful steeds) to a blacksmith's forge and had them shod with gold. And when they had had them shod, they rode up to the castle. By the wee red fellow's order, they didn't wait to knock at any gates, but put their golden spurs to their horses and leaped them over the castle walls.

When the servants and soldiers saw the pair come bounding over the castle walls upon horses shod with gold, they ran out in wonder. From the Purse of Plenty the red fellow, as Jack's servant, pulled out handfuls and handfuls of silver and of gold and scattered them among the crowd.

Then the servants quickly brought word to the Princess of the East of the beautiful and rich gentleman who had come, with his servant, to court her. They told her how they had both leaped the castle walls on horses shod with gold, and that they threw away their gold in handfuls.

She sent word for Jack to be brought to her, and when Jack came into her presence, he was enchanted with the look of her; for her hair was so black, her cheeks and lips were so red, and her skin was so white, he had never seen in all his life any one so beautiful.

She took him into the Garden of Heads and showed
him three hundred and sixty-five rose bushes.

The Snow, Crow, and Blood

"I understand you have come to court me," says she.

"That I have," says Jack.

"Well," says she, "to every one that comes to court me, I give three tasks. If any one performs the three tasks I give him he will win me; but if he fails in any one of the three, he will lose his head. Are you willing to try on such conditions?" says she.

"I'll try," says Jack, "upon any conditions."

She took him out then into the Garden of Heads, and showed him three hundred and sixty-five rose bushes, and for every flower there was a man's head on every one of three hundred and sixty-four of the bushes.

"There's one bush without a flower yet, Jack," says she, "but in less than three days I hope to see your head flowering on it."

Then she took him into the castle again, and treated him to a fine supper. And when they had finished supper and drunk their wine and chatted, she got up to bid him good-night.

She took out of her hair a gold comb, and showed it to him. "Now," she says, "I will wear that golden comb all night, and I'll spend this night from midnight to cockcrow neither on the earth nor under the earth. Yet you must have that comb for me in the morning, and it must be taken from my head between midnight and cockcrow." Then she stuck the comb into her hair again and went off.

Poor Jack acknowledged to himself that he had a task before him which he couldn't do. He wandered down the stairs and out of the castle, and went meandering into the garden in low spirits.

The wee red man soon came to him and asked him what was the matter.

"Oh, matter enough," says Jack, and commenced telling him all.

"Keep up your heart," says the wee red man, "and I'll see what I can do for you."

So the little red man went and got his Cloak of Darkness, and then watched till midnight outside the Princess's door.

Just one second before the stroke of midnight, the Princess came out of her room with the golden comb in her hair, and went off to Hell. The little red man threw his Cloak of Darkness around him, and followed her.

She didn't stop till she came to Hell, where she went in, and the little red man went in after her.

The Devil was very glad to see her, and he

The wee red man came up
behind and snatched the
gold comb out of her hair.

The Snow, Crow, and Blood

kissed her, and the two sat down side by side and began to chat.   And as they couldn't see the wee red man for his Cloak of Darkness, he came up behind and snatched the gold comb out of her hair, and went off with it ; and when he came to earth, he gave the comb to Jack.

In the morning when the Princess of the East appeared at breakfast, Jack handed her her gold comb across the table.   She was furious, and the eyes of her flashed fire.   That night she showed him a diamond ring on her finger, and she said she would not be on earth or under the earth between midnight and cockcrow, yet he must get that ring between those two times, and have it for her in the morning.

And when she went away, Jack went down to the garden, and was wandering about there when the wee red man came up to him and asked him what was the matter, and he told the wee red man.

"Well," says the wee red man, "I'll try what I can do."   And so he took his Cloak of Darkness and watched for her that night again, and just before midnight, she came out and went off.   He followed her, and she didn't stop till she was in Hell, where the Devil was very glad to see her and kissed her, and they sat down side by side to chat.

The little red fellow, with his Cloak of Darkness, came up beside her and waited, and the first opportunity he got, he snatched the ring off her finger, and went off and gave it to Jack.

So when she came down to breakfast the next morning Jack handed her over the table her diamond ring; and this morning she was doubly as furious as on the morning before. "Well," she said, "you've done two of the tasks, but the third you never will do."

So that night she told him: "I will spend all the time between midnight and cockcrow neither on the earth nor under the earth; and I want you to have for me in the morning the lips I shall have kissed while I have been away. Your head I'll surely have now, for the sword was never yet made by mortal man that can cut those lips."

Then she went away.

Poor Jack, he wandered out into the garden very down-hearted at this, and sure and certain that he would lose his head in the morning.

The little red man came up to him and asked him what was the matter. Jack told, him and the red fellow said: "Keep up your heart, and

The Snow, Crow, and Blood

I'll see what can be done." And he reminded Jack that he had the Sword of Light, which was never made by mortal man.

He threw his Cloak of Darkness about him, took the Sword of Light with him, and watched by the Princess's door. Just before midnight she came out and went off, and he followed her to Hell, where the Devil welcomed her with a kiss, and as he did so the little red man raised the Sword of Light and cut the lips off of him and went off as fast as he could.

So in the morning Jack handed them across the table to the Princess, who was shaking with rage, and then he demanded her hand in marriage. And she had to consent.

As soon as they were married, the little red man said to Jack: "I have a wedding present for you." So he gave him ten blackthorns and told him to break one of these blackthorns on his wife every morning for ten mornings, and if he followed out his instructions faithfully, he would have a good wife on the tenth day.

Seeing the little red man had been such a good friend to him, Jack consented to do this. He broke a blackthorn on her every morning for ten mornings, and for every blackthorn he broke on her she was dispossessed of a devil. And on

Donegal fairy Stories

the tenth day she had lost all her rage and all her fury and all the devils, and she was the best and most perfect girl, as well as the most beautiful one, in all the world.

The little red man on the tenth day asked Jack if he remembered when he set out on his travels paying a hundred guineas to get a corpse buried. Jack said he did.

"Then," said the little red man, "it was I whom you buried, and I have tried to repay you a little. Now, good-bye, and may you and your wife prosper ever after."

The little red man disappeared, and Jack and his beautiful wife lived long and happily.

The Adventures of Ciad, Son of the
King of Norway

The Adventures of Ciad, Son of the King of Norway

IAD, Ceud, and Mith-Ceud were the three sons of the King of Norway. All over the world they were celebrated as fine, brave fellows, and they had come to think themselves so, too.

On a day after Ciad had been walking by the shore for a long time, thinking, he came back to his father's castle. He said to his father and his brothers: "Ceud and Mith-Ceud and Ciad are celebrated far and wide as great heroes and gallant champions, but I have just been thinking, do we deserve this? Neither of us has ever done anything great. I think it is not right to bear the name of champion without having done something to earn it. I will leave my father's castle, and go away and prove my right to the title of hero, or, if I fail, I will never come back."

Donegal fairy Stories

The King of Norway tried hard to persuade him not to go, but Ciad would not be persuaded. He said: "I am sorely ashamed of myself for bearing a title that I have not deserved."

Then, when the King found that Ciad was bent on going, he asked him to take the pick of his men to accompany him on his adventures.

Ciad said: "No, I'll go by myself."

The King could not induce him to take any men.

Early next morning Ciad was up and breakfasted. He took his arms and his shield with him, and started off. He went to the seashore, and traveled away and away, along it.

When he had been traveling for three hours, he saw a speck far out at sea, but it was coming nearer and getting bigger every minute. At last he saw it was a boat, and when it came still nearer, he saw that a woman sat in it. When it was nearer still, he saw that she was a very beautiful lady.

He stood his ground, as the boat was coming straight toward him. At length the boat's keel grated on the gravel, and Ciad helped the young lady on shore. He said: " Beautiful lady, who are you? Where do you come from? Or where do you go all alone?"

At length the boat's keel
grated on the ground.

The Adventures of Ciad

"Before I answer that," she said, "give me your name; for I will not reply to those questions unless you are of royal blood."

He said: "I am of royal blood. I am Ciad, son of the King of Norway."

She said: "I am glad of that. I am Dark Eye, the daughter of the King of France. From France I have come, but where I am going I do not know. For a year and a day I have been wandering over the seas in this little boat, seeking 'for a champion. A cruel stepmother has laid a spell on me, under which I have to leave home, and must wander forever and ever over the seas and the oceans in this little boat, unless I can find for her the bottle of loca [loca was a balm that could instantly cure all wounds, and even restore life itself to the dead] that is owned by the Queen of the Island of the Riches of the World. When I find that, my stepmother's spell will be lifted off me. For three years now I have been wandering over the world seeking for this island, but cannot find it, and can find no one who knows where it is. I have already put geasa on the twelve greatest champions of the world, ordering them to bring me this bottle. None of them got it, but instead the twelve lost their lives. As you are a King's son and a hero,

Donegal fairy Stories

I put geasa upon you to bring me this bottle of loca of the Queen of the Island of the Riches of the World, and hand it to me on this spot in three years and a day from now.

Ciad said: "I accept the geasa, Dark Eye."

Dark Eye thanked him. He helped her into her boat; she pushed off, and sailed away and away until he lost sight of her. Then Ciad turned and walked back to his father's castle. He told his father of his adventure and of the geasa that had been laid on him.

"My poor boy," his father said, "I am very sorry for you. There are not three in all the world who know where the Island of the Riches of the World is, and even if you could find that, you would lose your life in trying to take the bottle of loca."

Ciad said that better men than he had already lost their lives in the search, so it would be no shame for him if he, too, lost his.

His father asked him to take nine times nine nines of men with him, if he was bent on fulfilling his geasa.

But Ciad said: "No. I shall not take nine men. Give me a ship, and let my brothers Ceud and Mith-Ceud go along with me. If it is possible to get the bottle of loca of the Queen of the

The Adventures of Ciad

Island of the Riches of the World, I, with Ceud
and Mith-Ceud, will get it. If it is impossible,
then your nine times nine nines of men would be
lost to you, as well as we."

His father gave him the best ship in the har-
bor, and with Ceud and Mith-Ceud, Ciad, on
the morrow, set out on his quest.

They sailed for two days and two nights without meeting any adventure; and on the third
day they saw a speck on the sea, far off. Very
soon they saw it was a ship coming towards
them. As they came nearer to it they found that
it was very large, and when they came very
near they saw that in the ship was one person, a
great giant, greater than any giant in Norway.

When the strange ship came up beside them,
the giant asked Ciad who he was and what
right he had to sail these waters.

Ciad said: "My name I'm not ashamed of. I
am Ciad, the son of the King of Norway, a hero.
Who are you, and by what right do you question me?"

He said: "I am the Giant of the Great Seas,
and I allow no ship upon these waters."

Said Ciad: "If that is your law I am sorry for
you, for it's going to be broken this day."

The giant raised his spear, and Ciad, without

Donegal Fairy Stories

waiting, leaped aboard the giant's ship with his spear in his hand and with his shield before him.

Ciad and the Giant of the Great Seas fell to, and fought as two men never fought before. Their fight was so loud and so fierce and so terrible that the seals came from the North Seas and the whales came from the deeps of the ocean, and the little red fishes came up from the sea-meadows and gathered around the ships to watch the fight. The giant was brave and a great fighter, without doubt; his strength and skill were wonderful; but the courageous spirit of Ciad was greater than the giant's strength and skill. When the sun was two hours above the Eastern waters they had begun the fight, and when it was going down into the Western waters the fight was not ended. But it was very nearly so, for the giant was weakening, and soon he would have been beaten, but he gave three calls, and a blue mist came down from the skies and wrapped his ship round.

When the mist cleared away, the giant and the ship were gone, and Ciad was struggling in the water.

Ceud and Mith-Ceud took him aboard and found he was so badly abused and so weak from fighting and loss of blood, that there was noth-

ing for it but to return home; so home they
went.

At home Ciad lay in his bed for three days,
with his father's doctors attending him. At the
end of that time he got up and asked his father
to give him thirty men and another ship, that he
might set out on his journey again.

His father tried to persuade him not to go, but
it was of no use. Ciad said if he did not fulfill
his geasa, he could never hold up his head with
men again.

Then he set out with two ships. Ceud, Mith-
Ceud, and himself were in one ship, and his
father's thirty men in the other.

They sailed for three days and three nights in
the same direction in which they had gone
before, and on the morning of the fourth day, he
saw two specks on the waters, far off. They
were coming towards him. They got larger
every moment. He saw they were two ships.
When they came nearer, he saw the giant standing in one, and a host of men in the other.
When they came quite close, Ciad hailed the
Giant of the Great Seas and asked him did he
mean battle.

The giant replied: "If you do not mean battle,
I do not."

Donegal Fairy Stories

"Where are you going, then?" Ciad asked.

The giant said: "I'm going in search of the Riches of the World."

"Where is that to be found?" said Ciad.

"It's on an island in the Far World," the giant said, "and is owned by the Queen of the Island of the Riches of the World."

"Then I'll go with you," Ciad said.

The giant agreed to this, and all sailed off.

They sailed away and away, far further than I could tell you, and twice as far as you could tell me, until at length they reached the island.

The giant said to Ciad: "Send your men on the island first, and demand the Riches of the World."

Ciad agreed to this, and sent his men on the island on a morning, but when night fell they had not come back. Next day Ciad himself landed, and went in search of them. In the second valley, he found his thirty men lying in blood. He said: "This is the giant's doing."

So he went back to his ship and told his two brothers if they would engage the giant's men, he would engage the giant himself. This was agreed to, and they attacked the giant and his men.

A fiercer and bloodier battle was never fought

He found his thirty men
lying in blood.

on sea or land. The noise and the din were so loud, and the battling was so fierce, that the seals came down from the North Seas, the whales up from the deeps of the ocean, and the little red fishes, too, from the sea-meadows, gathering around the ship to watch the fight. For the length of a day they battled, and when the sun was one hour above the Western waters, Ceud, Mith-Ceud, and the giant's men were all of them dead, but Ciad and the giant still battled. When the hoop of the sun was on the waters, the giant, finding himself weakening too fast, gave three calls. Ciad saw the blue mist coming down; he gave a bound into the air and drove his spear to the giant's heart, and killed him.

Then he went on the island, and stood his two brothers up against a rock facing the east, with helmets on their heads, and shields and spears in their hands. On the next morning he set out to travel over the island, and at night he came to a little hut, where he found one old hag. He asked her if she had no company.

She said: "Yes, I have plenty of that."

He asked to see her company.

She struck her staff on the hearthstone, and up sprang nine other hags as old and as ugly as herself. She struck the staff again upon the hearthstone, and then they were the nine most beautiful damsels Ciad had ever seen.

The hag said : "If you stay with me, you can have your choice of these nine beautiful damsels for your wife."

But Ciad remembered Dark Eye of France, and also remembered his geasa, and he said to the hag, he would have none of them.

Then she struck her staff upon the ground angrily, and they all disappeared.

He asked for supper and a bed for the night, and the old hag gave him the toes and the tongue of a rabbit for supper. She gave him a heather bed that scored and cut him, and an old black cat for a bedfellow.

In the morning he told the hag that he was looking for the queen of this island.

She said : "I am the queen."

"If that is so," he said, "I demand the bottle of loca and the Riches of the World."

"That," she said, "I am glad you cannot have."

"If I cannot have it," he said, "I will take your staff and break your old bones."

"It's like a hero to do that," she said scoffingly ; but even if you made meal of my old

The Adventures of Ciad

bones, you would not be nearer the bottle of loca and the Riches of the World."

Ciad asked how that was.

She said : " Feach-An-Chruic [the Terrible Man of the Hill] took away the bottle of loca and the Riches of the World from me two hundred years ago."

" I do not believe it," said Ciad.

But she took him outside and showed him the hoof tracks of the Feach's horses, where last night's rains were still lying in them.

" Where does Feach-An-Chruic live? " Ciad asked.

" He lives a third part of the world from here," the hag said.

" How may I get there? " Ciad said.

" As best you can," said the hag.

" By this and by that," said Ciad, seizing her staff, " I'll make meal of your old bones if you don't direct me."

She took him down to the shore, took a black whistle from her pocket and blew on it, when a little red fish appeared on top of the water.

"There," she said, "follow that fish, and it will lead you to Feach-An-Chruic."

Ciad stepped into his ship, hoisted his sails, and went off after the little red fish.

Donegal Fairy Stories

He went away for long, long days and long, long nights, sailing one-third of the whole world, until at length the little fish ran into a wood-bordered bay. Ciad anchored his ship here, and went on shore.

He traveled over the mountains for three days and three nights, and on the fourth day he found Feach-An-Chruic dividing beef among his men.

Ciad walked up to him, and asked for a bit of the beef.

"By my faith, no!" said Feach-An-Chruic. "But now that you're here I'll save my beef."

"How is that?" said Ciad.

"Because I'll divide you among my men," said Feach-An-Chruic.

"You might not," said Ciad.

So Ciad and the Feach fell to and fought.

The Feach was a wild and terrible fighter surely, but the courageous spirit of Ciad made him a better. The noise and din and fierceness of the fight was so great that the boars came down from the hills, and the deer came up from the valleys, and the birds came from the woods of the world, to watch it; but before night fell Ciad put the Feach down. Then he put his knee on his breast, and asked him where he

The Adventures of Ciad

would find the bottle of Ioca and the Riches of the World.

Feach-An-Chruic said: "If that is what you came for and what you fought for, I'm sorry for you. I had the bottle of Ioca and the Riches of the World only one night when Feach-An-Choille [the Terrible Man of the Wood] took them from me."

"I do not believe it," said Ciad.

But the Feach showed him the footprints of Feach-An-Choille, with last night's rains still lying in them.

"And where does Feach-An-Choille live?" said Ciad.

"He lives a third of the world from here," said Feach-An-Chruic.

"And how may I get there?" Ciad asked.

"You're a brave man," said Feach-An-Chruic, "and I would like to see you succeed."

With the point of his spear he rang three times on his shield, and a wolf-dog came running up. "Follow that dog," said Feach-An-Chruic, "and he will lead you to Feach-An-Choille."

Ciad set out after the dog, and he traveled away and away, far further than I could tell you, and twice as far as you could tell me, over hill, height, and hollow, mountain, moor, and scrug, lone valley and green glen, for long and for long, until at length and at last he reached the land of Feach-An-Choille. Traveling through it he came upon a hut, and saw Feach-An-Choille himself standing outside. He was leaning against the end of his hut laughing, and every time he laughed oak trees fell.

"Why do you laugh?" said Ciad, when he reached him.

"I'm laughing for the joy of killing you," said Feach-An-Choille.

"Wouldn't it be better to laugh after?" said Ciad.

Then he raised his spear, and he and the Feach went at the fight. The noise and the din and the fierceness of the fight was such that the boars came down from the hills, and the deer came up from the valleys, and the birds from the woods of the world loaded the tree tops around, to watch. If Feach-An-Chruic was a great fighter, Feach-An-Choille was a far greater, but as great as he was, Ciad's courageous spirit was still greater, and when the sun was behind the trees in the west, Ciad put the Feach down.

"You're a brave man," said the Feach, when he was down. "What can I do for you?"

The boars and the deer and
the birds all came to watch
it.

The Adventures of Ciad

"You can give me the bottle of Ioca and the Riches of the World," said Ciad.

"I cannot," said the Feach. "I'm sorry. I had the bottle of Ioca and the Riches of the World only one night, when the King of Persia took them from me. And now," said the Feach, "you may as well return home, for you can never get them from the King of Persia."

"Why cannot I?" said Ciad.

"Because," he said, "the King of Persia, when he got the Riches of the World, called together at once the Seven Wizards of the East, and had them lay spells on him, so that no man could ever conquer him."

"I'm sorry for that," said Ciad, "but I'll not return home; I'll travel on to meet my fate."

Ciad traveled on for a long time. He came to a plain that was covered with dead men, and on one of the dead men he saw a gold boot and a silver boot. He got hold of the gold boot and tried to pull it off, and the man whom he thought was dead struck him with the other boot and tossed him.

"Who are you?" said Ciad.

"I am Swift Sword, son of the King of Spain, one blow of whose sword has the power of one thousand men for one thousand years, and would blow the sea dry," he said. "This is my army that I brought into the Eastern World, and all of them are killed."

"I am glad to find you," said Ciad, "for I am your cousin Ciad, the son of the King of Norway. Come with me."

Ciad and Swift Sword set out, and traveled on and on until they came to the lake of the Singing Shore, and traveled by it until they reached a small house. As they came up to the house they saw a white pigeon fly from the chimney at every step they took.

Ciad thought this very strange and that he would go in and find out what it meant. Inside he saw a very beautiful young lady sitting by the fire. She had in her hand a wand covered with scales. She was plucking the scales from it, one by one, and flinging them into the fire, and for every scale she flung into the fire a white pigeon got up and flew from the chimney.

"The blessing of Crom on you," said Ciad. "I am Ciad, the son of the King of Norway. I am traveling in search of the King of Persia, to get from him the bottle of Ioca and the Riches of the World. I should like to know the name of the beautiful damsel I am addressing."

She said, "I am Pearl Mouth, daughter of the

for every scale she flung into the fire a white pigeon got up and flew into the chimney.

The Adventures of Ciad

King of Persia, and am living here all alone, very far from my country and my people."

" How is that?" said Ciad.

She said: "A year ago I married Blue Gold, the son of the King of Africa, and on my marriage day he was carried away by force by Mountain of Fierceness, son of the King of Greece, and turned into a pigeon in the Eastern Skies. I have sat here for a year sending off these messengers to find him, but not one of them has come back."

" I am very sorry for you," said Ciad.

"And I am very sorry for you," said Pearl Mouth.

" How is that?" said Ciad.

" Because my father, the King of Persia," she said, "cannot be conquered by living man; so you can never force from him the bottle of Ioca and the Riches of the World."

" Then I'll die in trying," said Ciad.

" Isn't it better to get them and live?" Pearl Mouth said.

" But I cannot do that," Ciad said.

" If you are a very great hero there is just a chance for you," said Pearl Mouth.

Ciad asked her what that chance was, and she told him that if he would find Mountain of

Donegal fairy Stories

Fierceness, the son of the King of Greece, and conquer him and bring back to her Blue Gold, she would get for him from her father what he wanted.

"Then," he said, "I will do that."

"Not so easily," said Pearl Mouth, "for no one in the world can overcome Mountain of Fierceness unless he has the buaidh* of Soul of Steel, Prince of India."

"Then," said Ciad, "I will set off and find that."

Away he started, and did not stop until he reached India. He demanded buaidh from Soul of Steel.

"That I will not give you," said Soul of Steel.

Then Ciad said, "I will fight you for it."

"You will only throw away your life," said Soul of Steel, "for no man can conquer me but one."

"And who is that one?" said Ciad.

"The man who can kill the Giant of the Great Seas," said Soul of Steel.

"Then," said Ciad, "I'm that man;" and he told his story to Soul of Steel.

Soul of Steel said he was a great hero, surely, and that he was glad to give him buaidh.

---

* Buaidh is pronounced "boo-ee," and means "power of victory."

The Adventures of Ciad

"Break a branch," he said, "from that oak tree that grows before my castle, and it will give you buaidh."

Ciad went to the oak tree and broke a branch, but when it fell to the ground, it sprang up into a great tree, and with every other branch he broke the same thing happened.

Soul of Steel came out and gave him his cloak. He said, "Spread this under the branch."

He broke another branch, which fell on the cloak, and he carried it off, and went in search of Mountain of Fierceness.

He traveled away and away before him, far further than I can tell you, and twice as far as you could tell me, over height, hill, and hollow, mountain, moor and scrug, lone valley and green glen, until at last and at length, he found, in Africa, Mountain of Fierceness with all his men, gathered together on a hilltop. He walked up to them, and asked what was happening.

They said Mountain of Fierceness was being married to the Queen of the Indies. He pushed his way to where the priests were marrying them.

Mountain of Fierceness asked the stranger what he wanted.

Ciad said, "I have come to conquer you."

Donegal fairy Stories

"That, my good man, you can't do," said Mountain of Fierceness. "It's better for you to return to your home, for I'm getting married."

"I'll never return until I've taken your life or made you grant me one request," said Ciad.

"I'll not give you my life, and I'll not grant you one request," said Mountain of Fierceness. "But I'll spit you on the point of my spear if you don't leave this and go whence you came."

Then Ciad asked him to step out for a fight.

"I don't want to take your life or any man's to-day," said Mountain of Fierceness, "as I am to be married. Yet no man can overcome me unless he has buaidh from Soul of Steel, the Prince of India."

"And that I have," said Ciad, throwing the oak branch at his feet.

Mountain of Fierceness looked at this, and then said: "Will you spare my life?"

"On one condition," said Ciad, "and that is that you tell me where Blue Gold, Prince of Africa, whom you carried off from his wife a year ago, is, and how I may get him."

"Where he is and what he is, I can tell you," said Mountain of Fierceness, "and how you may get him, but I very much doubt if ever you can get him. He is a wild pigeon in the Eastern

The Adventures of Ciad

Skies—nothing can catch him but the magic net of the King of Ireland's Druid, and this net could only be purchased by one-third of the Riches of the World; and nothing can disenchant him but nine grains of wheat that lie at the bottom of the Well of the World's End, which can only be emptied by three thousand men in three thousand years."

When Ciad heard this he bade him good-by. He sent Swift Sword to Ireland to get the loan of the magic net of the King of Ireland's Druid, on the promise of paying him one-third of the Riches of the World, and told Swift Sword to meet him at the Well of the World's End.

Away and away then he traveled, far further than I can tell you, and twice as far as you can tell me. Over hills a hundred miles high, and valleys a hundred miles deep ; across plains where living man had never been before, and through great woods that were so far from the world that the birds themselves had never reached them, until at length and at last he reached the Well of the World's End and there he found Swift Sword before him, with the net of the King of Ireland's Druid.

With three blows of the sword Swift Sword blew the Well of the World's End dry, and they took from the bottom the nine grains of wheat. They spread the net in the Eastern World and caught in it a hundred thousand pigeons, amongst them one great wild pigeon, which was Blue Gold.

They gave him to eat the nine grains of wheat, and there stood up a handsome prince before them—Blue Gold.

With him they traveled back away and away, until they came to the Lake of the Singing Shore, and to the little house where they found Pearl Mouth, who was rejoiced to get her Blue Gold back again.

Then the four of them set out, and traveled away and away, over mountains and valleys and great long plains, until they came to her father, the King of Persia, from whom she demanded the bottle of Ioca and the Riches of the World to give them to Ciad and repay him for his services.

The King of Persia said : " No man could ever take these from me, but I give them willingly to the brave champion, Ciad."

He and Swift Sword spent that night in the King of Persia's castle, and in the morning set out for home. When they came to the Plain of Blood, they shook one drop from the bottle of

Over mountains and val-
leys until they came to her
father's house.

The Adventures of Ciad

Ioca on Swift Sword's army, and all of them stood up alive and well.

Ciad then parted with Swift Sword, who was going on to conquer the East, and he himself—for his time was now getting short—did not turn aside, but went direct for home. And on the evening of the day on which the three years and a day would have expired, Ciad stood upon the spot on the seashore from which he had set out, and there he found Dark Eye awaiting him.

He gave her the bottle of Ioca, and her stepmother's spells were at once taken off her. They went to the island on which he had left his two brothers, Ceud and Mith-Ceud; he shook on them one drop from the bottle of Ioca, and the two were again alive and well. All of them set out, and sailed to Ciad's father's castle—he and his two brothers and Dark Eye, with the bottle of Ioca and the Riches of the World.

A messenger was sent at once to France, to invite the King to come to his daughter's marriage, and to bring his sons and his great lords with him. And another messenger brought to the King of Ireland's Druid his magic net and a third of the Riches of the World, and invited the King of Ireland and all his court to come to the marriage also.   One hundred kings sat down to the wedding feast.   The wedding lasted ninety-nine days and ninety-nine nights, and the last night was better than the first.

Ciad and Dark Eye lived a long life and a happy one, and may you and I do the same.

The Bee, the Harp, the Mouse, and the Bum-Clock

The Bee, the Harp, the Mouse, and the Bum-Clock

ONCE there was a widow, and she had one son, called Jack. Jack and his mother owned just three cows. They lived well and happy for a long time ; but at last hard times came down on them, and the crops failed, and poverty looked in at the door, and things got so sore against the poor widow that for want of money and for want of necessities she had to make up her mind to sell one of the cows. "Jack," she said one night, "go over in the morning to the fair to sell the branny cow."

Well and good: in the morning my brave Jack was up early, and took a stick in his fist and turned out the cow, and off to the fair he went with her; and when Jack came into the fair, he saw a great crowd gathered in a ring in the street. He went into the crowd to see what they were looking at, and there in the middle of them he saw a man with a wee, wee harp, a mouse, and a bum-clock [cockroach], and a bee to play the harp. And when the man put them down on the ground and whistled, the bee began to play the harp, and the mouse and the bum-clock stood up on their hind legs and got hold of each other and began to waltz. And as soon as the harp began to play and the mouse and the bum-clock to dance, there wasn't a man or woman, or a thing in the fair, that didn't begin to dance also ; and the pots and pans, and the wheels and reels jumped and jigged, all over the town, and Jack himself and the branny cow were as bad as the next.

There was never a town in such a state before or since, and after a while the man picked up the bee, the harp, and the mouse, and the bum-clock and put them into his pocket, and the men and women, Jack and the cow, the pots and pans, wheels and reels, that had hopped and jigged, now stopped, and every one began to laugh as if to break its heart. Then the man turned to Jack. "Jack," says he, "how would you like to be master of all these animals ?"

"Why," says Jack, "I should like it fine."

Off to the fair he went
with her.

The Bee, Harp, Mouse, Bum-Clock

" Well, then," says the man, " how will you and me make a bargain about them ?"

" I have no money," says Jack.

" But you have a fine cow," says the man. " I will give you the bee and the harp for it."

" O, but," Jack says, says he, " my poor mother at home is very sad and sorrowful entirely, and I have this cow to sell and lift her heart again."

" And better than this she cannot get," says the man. " For when she sees the bee play the harp, she will laugh if she never laughed in her life before."

"Well," says Jack, says he, "that will be grand."

He made the bargain. The man took the cow ; and Jack started home with the bee and the harp in his pocket, and when he came home, his mother welcomed him back.

" And Jack," says she, " I see you have sold the cow."

" I have done that," says Jack.

" Did you do well ?" says the mother.

" I did well, and very well," says Jack.

" How much did you get for her ?" says the mother.

" O," says he, " it was not for money at all I sold her, but for something far better."

Donegal Fairy Stories

"O, Jack! Jack!" says she, "what have you done?"

"Just wait until you see, mother," says he, "and you will soon say I have done well."

Out of his pocket he takes the bee and the harp and sets them in the middle of the floor, and whistles to them, and as soon as he did this the bee began to play the harp, and the mother she looked at them and let a big, great laugh out of her, and she and Jack began to dance, the pots and pans, the wheels and reels began to jig and dance over the floor, and the house itself hopped about also.

When Jack picked up the bee and the harp again the dancing all stopped, and the mother laughed for a long time. But when she came to herself, she got very angry entirely with Jack, and she told him he was a silly, foolish fellow, that there was neither food nor money in the house, and now he had lost one of her good cows also. "We must do something to live," says she. "Over to the fair you must go to-morrow morning, and take the black cow with you and sell her."

And off in the morning at an early hour brave Jack started, and never halted until he was in the fair. When he came into the fair, he saw a

Cbe Bee, Mouse, Darp, Bum-Clock

big crowd gathered in a ring in the street. Said Jack to himself, " I wonder what are they looking at."

Into the crowd he pushed, and saw the wee man this day again with a mouse and a bum-clock, and he put them down in the street and whistled. The mouse and the bum-clock stood up on their hind legs and got hold of each other and began to dance there and jig, and as they did there was not a man or woman in the street who didn't begin to jig also, and Jack and the black cow, and the wheels and the reels, and the pots and pans, all of them were jigging and dancing all over the town, and the houses themselves were jumping and hopping about, and such a place Jack or any one else never saw before.

When the man lifted the mouse and the bum-clock into his pocket, they all stopped dancing and settled down, and everybody laughed right hearty. The man turned to Jack. "Jack," said he, "I am glad to see you ; how would you like to have these animals ?"

" I should like well to have them," says Jack, says he, " only I cannot."

"Why cannot you?" says the man.

" O," says Jack, says he, "I have no money,

and my poor mother is very down-hearted. She sent me to the fair to sell this cow and bring some money to lift her heart."

"O," says the man, says he, "if you want to lift your mother's heart I will sell you the mouse, and when you set the bee to play the harp and the mouse to dance to it, your mother will laugh if she never laughed in her life before."

"But I have no money," says Jack, says he, "to buy your mouse."

"I don't mind," says the man, says he, "I will take your cow for it."

Poor Jack was so taken with the mouse and had his mind so set on it, that he thought it was a grand bargain entirely, and he gave the man his cow, and took the mouse and started off for home, and when he got home his mother welcomed him.

"Jack," says she, "I see you have sold the cow."

"I did that," says Jack.

"Did you sell her well?" says she.

"Very well indeed," says Jack, says he.

"How much did you get for her?"

"I didn't get money," says he, "but I got value."

The Bee, Mouse, Harp, Bum-Clock

" O, Jack ! Jack !" says she, "what do you mean ?"

" I will soon show you that, mother," says he, taking the mouse out of his pocket and the harp and the bee and setting all on the floor ; and when he began to whistle the bee began to play, and the mouse got up on its hind legs and began to dance and jig, and the mother gave such a hearty laugh as she never laughed in her life before. To dancing and jigging herself and Jack fell, and the pots and pans and the wheels and reels began to dance and jig over the floor, and the house jigged also. And when they were tired of this, Jack lifted the harp and the mouse and the bee and put them in his pocket, and his mother she laughed for a long time.

But when she got over that she got very downhearted and very angry entirely with Jack. " And O, Jack," she says, " you are a stupid, good-for-nothing fellow. We have neither money nor meat in the house, and here you have lost two of my good cows, and I have only one left now. To-morrow morning," she says, " you must be up early and take this cow to the fair and sell her. See to get something to lift my heart up."

Donegal Fairy Stories

"I will do that," says Jack, says he. So he went to his bed, and early in the morning he was up and turned out the spotty cow and went to the fair.

When Jack got to the fair, he saw a crowd gathered in a ring in the street. "I wonder what they are looking at, anyhow," says he. He pushed through the crowd, and there he saw the same wee man he had seen before, with a bum-clock; and when he put the bum-clock on the ground, he whistled, and the bum-clock began to dance, and the men, women, and children in the street, and Jack and the spotty cow began to dance and jig also, and everything on the street and about it, the wheels and reels, the pots and pans, began to jig, and the houses themselves began to dance likewise. And when the man lifted the bum-clock and put it in his pocket, everybody stopped jigging and dancing and every one laughed loud. The wee man turned, and saw Jack.

"Jack, my brave boy," says he, "you will never be right fixed until you have this bum-clock, for it is a very fancy thing to have."

"O, but," says Jack, says he, "I have no money."

"No matter for that," says the man; "you

The Bee, Mouse, Harp, Bum-Clock

have a cow, and that is as good as money to me."

"Well," says Jack, "I have a poor mother who is very down-hearted at home, and she sent me to the fair to sell this cow and raise some money and lift her heart."

"O, but Jack," says the wee man, "this bum-clock is the very thing to lift her heart, for when you put down your harp and bee and mouse on the floor, and put the bum-clock along with them, she will laugh if she never laughed in her life before."

"Well, that is surely true," says Jack, says he, "and I think I will make a swap with you."

So Jack gave the cow to the man and took the bum-clock himself, and started for home. His mother was glad to see Jack back, and says she, "Jack, I see that you have sold the cow."

"I did that, mother," says Jack.

"Did you sell her well, Jack?" says the mother.

"Very well indeed, mother," says Jack.

"How much did you get for her?" says the mother.

"I didn't take any money for her, mother, but value," says Jack, and he takes out of his pocket the bum-clock and the mouse, and set them on the floor and began to whistle, and the bee began to play the harp and the mouse and the bum-clock stood up on their hind legs and began to dance, and Jack's mother laughed very hearty, and everything in the house, the wheels and the reels, and the pots and pans, went jigging and hopping over the floor, and the house itself went jigging and hopping about likewise.

When Jack lifted up the animals and put them in his pocket, everything stopped, and the mother laughed for a good while. But after a while, when she came to herself, and saw what Jack had done and how they were now without either money, or food, or a cow, she got very, very angry at Jack, and scolded him hard, and then sat down and began to cry.

Poor Jack, when he looked at himself, confessed that he was a stupid fool entirely. " And what," says he, " shall I now do for my poor mother?" He went out along the road, thinking and thinking, and he met a wee woman who said, " Good-morrow to you. Jack," says she, " how is it you are not trying for the King's daughter of Ireland?"

" What do you mean?" says Jack.

Says she : " Didn't you hear what the whole world has heard, that the King of Ireland has a

"What heads are these?"
Jack asked.

The Bee, Harp, Mouse, Bum-Clock

daughter who hasn't laughed for seven years, and he has promised to give her in marriage, and to give the kingdom along with her, to any man who will take three laughs out of her."

" If that is so," says Jack, says he, " it is not here I should be."

Back to the house he went, and gathers together the bee, the harp, the mouse, and the bum-clock, and putting them into his pocket, he bade his mother good-by, and told her it wouldn't be long till she got good news from him, and off he hurries.

When he reached the castle, there was a ring of spikes all round the castle and men's heads on nearly every spike there.

" What heads are these ?" Jack asked one of the King's soldiers.

" Any man that comes here trying to win the King's daughter, and fails to make her laugh three times, loses his head and has it stuck on a spike. These are the heads of the men that failed," says he.

"A mighty big crowd," says Jack, says he. Then Jack sent word to tell the King's daughter and the King that there was a new man who had come to win her.

In a very little time the King and the King's

daughter and the King's court all came out and sat themselves down on gold and silver chairs in front of the castle, and ordered Jack to be brought in until he should have his trial. Jack, before he went, took out of his pocket the bee, the harp, the mouse, and the bum-clock, and he gave the harp to the bee, and he tied a string to one and the other, and took the end of the string himself, and marched into the castle yard before all the court, with his animals coming on a string behind him.

When the Queen and the King and the court and the princes saw poor ragged Jack with his bee, and mouse, and bum-clock hopping behind him on a string, they set up one roar of laughter that was long and loud enough, and when the King's daughter herself lifted her head and looked to see what they were laughing at, and saw Jack and his paraphernalia, she opened her mouth and she let out of her such a laugh as was never heard before.

Then Jack dropped a low courtesy, and said, "Thank you, my lady ; I have one of the three parts of you won."

Then he drew up his animals in a circle, and began to whistle, and the minute he did, the bee began to play the harp, and the mouse and the

The Bee, Harp, Mouse, Bum-Clock

bum-clock stood up on their hind legs, got hold of each other, and began to dance, and the King and the King's court and Jack himself began to dance and jig, and everything about the King's castle, pots and pans, wheels and reels and the castle itself began to dance also. And the King's daughter, when she saw this, opened her mouth again, and let out of her a laugh twice louder than she let before, and Jack, in the middle of his jigging, drops another courtesy, and says, "Thank you, my lady; that is two of the three parts of you won."

Jack and his menagerie went on playing and dancing, but Jack could not get the third laugh out of the King's daughter, and the poor fellow saw his big head in danger of going on the spike. Then the brave mouse came to Jack's help and wheeled round upon its heel, and as it did so its tail swiped into the bum-clock's mouth, and the bum-clock began to cough and cough and cough. And when the King's daughter saw this she opened her mouth again, and she let the loudest and hardest and merriest laugh that was ever heard before or since ; and, "Thank you, my lady," says Jack, dropping another courtesy; "I have all of you won."

Then when Jack stopped his menagerie, the

Donegal Fairy Stories

King took himself and the menagerie within the castle. He was washed and combed, and dressed in a suit of silk and satin, with all kinds of gold and silver ornaments, and then was led before the King's daughter. And true enough she confessed that a handsomer and finer fellow than Jack she had never seen, and she was very willing to be his wife.

Jack sent for his poor old mother and brought her to the wedding, which lasted nine days and nine nights, every night better than the other. All the lords and ladies and gentry of Ireland were at the wedding. I was at it, too, and got brogues, broth and slippers of bread and came jigging home on my head.

The Old Hag's Long Leather Bag

The Old Hag's Long Leather Bag

ONCE on a time, long, long ago, there was a widow woman who had three daughters. When their father died, their mother thought they never would want, for he had left her a long leather bag filled with gold and silver. But he was not long dead, when an old Hag came begging to the house one day and stole the long leather bag filled with gold and silver, and went away out of the country with it, no one knew where.

So from that day, the widow woman and her three daughters were poor, and she had a hard struggle to live and to bring up her three daughters.

But when they were grown up, the eldest said one day : "Mother, I'm a young woman now, and it's a shame for me to be here doing nothing to help you or myself. Bake me a bannock and cut me a callop, till I go away to push my fortune."

The mother baked her a whole bannock, and asked her if she would have half of it with her blessing or the whole of it without. She said to give her the whole bannock without.

So she took it and went away. She told them if she was not back in a year and a day from that, then they would know she was doing well, and making her fortune.

She traveled away and away before her, far further than I could tell you, and twice as far as you could tell me, until she came into a strange country, and going up to a little house, she found an old Hag living in it. The Hag asked her where she was going. She said she was going to push her fortune.

Said the Hag : "How would you like to stay here with me, for I want a maid ?"

"What will I have to do ?" said she.

"You will have to wash me and dress me, and sweep the hearth clean; but on the peril of your life, never look up the chimney," said the Hag.

"All right," she agreed to this.

The next day, when the Hag arose, she wash-

But she flung a stone at
him and went on.

The Old Hag's Long Leather Bag

ed her and dressed her, and when the Hag went out, she swept the hearth clean, and she thought it would be no harm to have one wee look up the chimney. And there what did she see but her own mother's long leather bag of gold and silver? So she took it down at once, and getting it on her back, started away for home as fast as she could run.

But she had not gone far when she met a horse grazing in a field, and when he saw her, he said: "Rub me! Rub me! for I haven't been rubbed these seven years."

But she only struck him with a stick she had in her hand, and drove him out of her way.

She had not gone much further when she met a sheep, who said: "O, shear me! Shear me! for I haven't been shorn these seven years."

But she struck the sheep, and sent it scurrying out of her way.

She had not gone much further when she met a goat tethered, and he said: "O, change my tether! Change my tether! for it hasn't been changed these seven years."

But she flung a stone at him, and went on.

Next she came to a lime-kiln, and it said: "O, clean me! Clean me! for I haven't been cleaned these seven years."

Donegal fairy Stories

But she only scowled at it, and hurried on.

After another bit she met a cow, and it said :
"O, milk me ! Milk me! for I haven't been milked these seven years."

She struck the cow out of her way, and went on.

Then she came to a mill. The mill said : "O, turn me ! Turn me ! for I haven't been turned these seven years."

But she did not heed what it said, only went in and lay down behind the mill door, with the bag under her head, for it was then night.

When the hag came into her hut again and found the girl gone, she ran to the chimney and looked up to see if she had carried off the bag. She got into a great rage, and she started to run as fast as she could after her.

She had not gone far when she met the horse, and she said : "O, horse, horse of mine, did you see this maid of mine, with my tig, with my tag, with my long leather bag, and all the gold and silver I have earned since I was a maid ?"

"Ay," said the horse, "it is not long since she passed here."

So on she ran, and it was not long till she met the sheep, and said she : "Sheep, sheep of mine,

O, horse, horse of mine,
did you see this maid of
mine?

The Old Hag's Long Leather Bag

did you see this maid of mine, with my tig, with my tag, with my long leather bag, and all the gold and silver I have earned since I was a maid ?"

"Ay," said the sheep, "it is not long since she passed here."

So she goes on, and it was not long before she met the goat, and said she : "Goat, goat of mine, did you see this maid of mine, with my tig, with my tag, with my long leather bag, and all the gold and silver I have earned since I was a maid ? "

" Ay," said the goat, " it is not long since she passed here."

So she goes on, and it was not long before she met the lime-kiln, and said she : "Lime-kiln, lime-kiln of mine, did you see this maid of mine, with my tig, with my tag, with my long leather bag, and with all the gold and silver I have earned since I was a maid ? "

" Ay," said the lime-kiln, "it is not long since she passed here."

So she goes on, and it was not long before she met the cow, and said she, "Cow, cow of mine, did you see this maid of mine, with my tig, with my tag, with my long leather bag, and all the gold and silver I have earned since I was a maid ? "

Donegal fairy Stories

"Ay," said the cow, "it is not long since she passed here."

So she goes on, and it was not long before she met the mill, and said she : "Mill, mill of mine, did you see this maid of mine, with my tig, with my tag, with my long leather bag, and all the gold and silver I have earned since I was a maid ?"

And the mill said : "Yes, she is sleeping behind the door."

She went in and struck her with a white rod, and turned her into a stone. She then took the bag of gold and silver on her back, and went away back home.

A year and a day had gone by after the eldest daughter left home, and when they found she had not returned, the second daughter got up, and she said : "My sister must be doing well and making her fortune, and isn't it a shame for me to be sitting here doing nothing, either to help you, mother, or myself. Bake me a bannock," said she, "and cut me a callop, till I go away to push my fortune."

The mother did this, and asked her would she have half the bannock with her blessing or the whole bannock without.

She said the whole bannock without, and she

The Old Hag's Long Leather Bag

set off. Then she said : " If I am not back here in a year and a day, you may be sure that I am doing well and making my fortune," and then she went away.

She traveled away and away on before her, far further than I could tell you, and twice as far as you could tell me, until she came into a strange country, and going up to a little house, she found an old Hag living in it. The old Hag asked her where she was going. She said she was going to push her fortune.

Said the Hag : "How would you like to stay here with me, for I want a maid ? "

"What will I have to do ? " says she.

"You'll have to wash me and dress me, and sweep the hearth clean; and on the peril of your life never look up the chimney," said the Hag.

"All right," she agreed to this.

The next day, when the Hag arose, she washed her and dressed her, and when the Hag went out she swept the hearth, and she thought it would be no harm to have one wee look up the chimney. And there what did she see but her own mother's long leather bag of gold and silver ? So she took it down at once, and getting it on her back, started away for home as fast as she could run.

Donegal Fairy Stories

But she had not gone far when she met a horse grazing in a field, and when he saw her, he said : " Rub me ! Rub me ! for I haven't been rubbed these seven years."

But she only struck him with a stick she had in her hand, and drove him out of her way.

She had not gone much further when she met the sheep, who said : " O, shear me ! Shear me ! for I haven't been shorn in seven years."

But she struck the sheep, and sent it scurrying out of her way.

She had not gone much further when she met the goat tethered, and he said : " O, change my tether ! Change my tether ! for it hasn't been changed in seven years."

But she flung a stone at him, and went on.

Next she came to the lime-kiln, and that said: " O, clean me ! Clean me ! for I haven't been cleaned these seven years."

But she only scowled at it, and hurried on.

Then she came to the cow, and it said : " O, milk me ! Milk me ! for I haven't been milked these seven years."

She struck the cow out of her way, and went on.

Then she came to the mill. The mill said : " O, turn me ! Turn me ! for I haven't been turned these seven years."

The Old Hag's Long Leather Bag

But she did not heed what it said, only went in and lay down behind the mill door, with the bag under her head, for it was then night.

When the Hag came into her hut again and found the girl gone, she ran to the chimney and looked up to see if she had carried off the bag. She got into a great rage, and she started to run as fast as she could after her.

She had not gone far when she met the horse, and she said: "O, horse, horse of mine, did you see this maid of mine, with my tig, with my tag, with my long leather bag, and all the gold and silver I have earned since I was a maid?"

"Ay," said the horse, "it is not long since she passed here."

So on she ran, and it was not long until she met the sheep, and said she: "Oh, sheep, sheep of mine, did you see this maid of mine, with my tig, with my tag, with my long leather bag, and all the gold and silver I have earned since I was a maid?"

"Ay," said the sheep, "it is not long since she passed here."

So she goes on, and it was not long before she met the goat, and said: "Goat, goat of mine, did you see this maid of mine, with my tig, with my tag, with my long leather bag, and all the gold and silver I have earned since I was a maid ?"

"Ay," said the goat, "it is not long since she passed here."

So she goes on, and it was not long before she met the lime-kiln, and said she : "Lime-kiln, lime-kiln of mine, did you see this maid of mine, with my tig, with my tag, with my long leather bag, and all the gold and silver I have earned since I was a maid ? "

"Ay," said the lime-kiln, "it is not long since she passed here."

So she goes on, and it was not long before she met the cow, and says she : "Cow, cow of mine, did you see this maid of mine, with my tig, with my tag, with my long leather bag, and all the gold and silver I have earned since I was a maid ? "

"Ay," said the cow, "it is not long since she passed here."

So she goes on, and it was not long before she met the mill, and said she : " Mill, mill of mine, did you see this maid of mine, with my tig, with my tag, with my long leather bag, and all the gold and silver I have earned since I was a maid ? "

And the mill said : "Yes, she is sleeping behind the door."

She struck her with her white rod and turned her into a stone.

The Old Hag's Long Leather Bag

She went in and struck her with a white rod, and turned her into a stone. She then took the bag of gold and silver on her back and went home.

When the second daughter had been gone a year and a day and she hadn't come back, the youngest daughter said : " My two sisters must be doing very well indeed, and making great fortunes when they are not coming back, and it's a shame for me to be sitting here doing nothing, either to help you, mother, or myself. Make me a bannock and cut me a callop, till I go away and push my fortune."

The mother did this and asked her would she have half of the bannock with her blessing or the whole bannock without.

She said : " I will have half of the bannock with your blessing, mother."

The mother gave her a blessing and half a bannock, and she set out.

She traveled away and away on before her, far further than I could tell you, and twice as far as you could tell me, until she came into a strange country, and going up to a little house, she found an old Hag living in it. The Hag asked her where she was going. She said she was going to push her fortune.

Donegal Fairy Stories

Said the Hag: "How would you like to stay here with me, for I want a maid?"

"What will I have to do?" said she.

"You'll have to wash me and dress me, and sweep the hearth clean; and on the peril of your life never look up the chimney," said the Hag.

"All right," she agreed to this.

The next day when the Hag arose, she washed her and dressed her, and when the Hag went out she swept the hearth, and she thought it would be no harm to have one wee look up the chimney, and there what did she see but her own mother's long leather bag of gold and silver? So she took it down at once, and getting it on her back, started away for home as fast as she could run.

When she got to the horse, the horse said: "Rub me! Rub me! for I haven't been rubbed these seven years."

"Oh, poor horse, poor horse," she said, "I'll surely do that." And she laid down her bag, and rubbed the horse.

Then she went on, and it wasn't long before she met the sheep, who said: "Oh, shear me, shear me! for I haven't been shorn these seven years."

"O, poor sheep, poor sheep," she said, "I'll

The Old Hag's Long Leather Bag

surely do that," and she laid down the bag, and sheared the sheep.

On she went till she met the goat, who said : "O, change my tether! Change my tether! for it hasn't been changed these seven years."

"O, poor goat, poor goat," she said, "I'll surely do that," and she laid down the bag, and changed the goat's tether.

Then she went on till she met the lime-kiln. The lime-kiln said : "O, clean me! Clean me! for I haven't been cleaned these seven years."

"O, poor lime-kiln, poor lime-kiln," she said, "I'll surely do that," and she laid down the bag and cleaned the lime-kiln.

Then she went on and met the cow. The cow said : "O, milk me! Milk me! for I haven't been milked these seven years."

"O, poor cow, poor cow," she said, "I'll surely do that," and she laid down the bag and milked the cow.

At last she reached the mill. The mill said : "O, turn me! turn me! for I haven't been turned these seven years."

"O, poor mill, poor mill," she said, "I'll surely do that," and she turned the mill too.

As night was on her, she went in and lay down behind the mill door to sleep.

Donegal Fairy Stories

When the Hag came into her hut again and found the girl gone, she ran to the chimney to see if she had carried off the bag. She got into a great rage, and started to run as fast as she could after her.

She had not gone far until she came up to the horse and said: "O, horse, horse of mine, did you see this maid of mine, with my tig, with my tag, with my long leather bag, and all the gold and silver I have earned since I was a maid?"

The horse said: "Do you think I have nothing to do only watch your maids for you? You may go somewhere else and look for information."

Then she came upon the sheep. "O, sheep, sheep of mine, have you seen this maid of mine, with my tig, with my tag, with my long leather bag, and all the gold and silver I have earned since I was a maid?"

The sheep said: "Do you think I have nothing to do only watch your maids for you? You may go somewhere else and look for information."

Then she went on till she met the goat. "O, goat, goat of mine, have you seen this maid of mine, with my tig, with my tag, with my long leather bag, and all the gold and silver I have earned since I was a maid?"

The mother was now ever
so glad to see them.

The Old Hag's Long Leather Bag

The goat said : "Do you think I have nothing to do only watch your maids for you ? You can go somewhere else and look for information."

Then she went on till she came to the lime-kiln. "O, lime-kiln, lime-kiln of mine, did you see this maid of mine, with my tig, with my tag, with my long leather bag, and all the gold and silver I have earned since I was a maid ?"

Said the lime-kiln : " Do you think I have nothing to do only to watch your maids for you ? You may go somewhere else and look for information."

Next she met the cow. " O, cow, cow of mine, have you seen this maid of mine, with my tig, with my tag, with my long leather bag, and all the gold and silver I have earned since I was a maid ? "

The cow said : " Do you think I have nothing to do only watch your maids for you ? You may go somewhere else and look for information."

Then she got to the mill. "O, mill, mill of mine, have you seen this maid of mine, with my tig, with my tag, with my long leather bag, and all the gold and silver I have earned since I was a maid ? "

The mill said : " Come nearer and whisper to me."

Donegal fairy Stories

She went nearer to whisper to the mill, and the mill dragged her under the wheels and ground her up.

The old Hag had dropped the white rod out of her hand, and the mill told the young girl to take this white rod and strike two stones behind the mill door. She did that, and her two sisters stood up. She hoisted the leather bag on her back, and the three of them set out and traveled away and away till they reached home.

The mother had been crying all the time while they were away, and was now ever so glad to see them, and rich and happy they all lived ever after.

A CATALOG OF SELECTED
DOVER BOOKS
IN ALL FIELDS OF INTEREST

A CATALOG OF SELECTED DOVER
BOOKS IN ALL FIELDS OF INTEREST

THE ART NOUVEAU STYLE, edited by Roberta Waddell. 579 rare photographs of works in jewelry, metalwork, glass, ceramics, textiles, architecture and furniture by 175 artists—Mucha, Seguy, Lalique, Tiffany, many others. 288pp. 8⅜ × 11¼.
23515-7 Pa. $9.95

AMERICAN COUNTRY HOUSES OF THE GILDED AGE (Sheldon's "Artistic Country-Seats"), A. Lewis. All of Sheldon's fascinating and historically important photographs and plans. New text by Arnold Lewis. Approx. 200 illustrations. 128pp. 9⅜ × 12¼.
24301-X Pa. $7.95

THE WAY WE LIVE NOW, Anthony Trollope. Trollope's late masterpiece, marks shift to bitter satire. Character Melmotte "his greatest villain." Reproduced from original edition with 40 illustrations. 416pp. 6⅛ × 9¼.
24360-5 Pa. $7.95

BENCHLEY LOST AND FOUND, Robert Benchley. Finest humor from early 30's, about pet peeves, child psychologists, post office and others. Mostly unavailable elsewhere. 73 illustrations by Peter Arno and others. 183pp. 5⅜ × 8½.
22410-4 Pa. $3.50

ISOMETRIC PERSPECTIVE DESIGNS AND HOW TO CREATE THEM, John Locke. Isometric perspective is the picture of an object adrift in imaginary space. 75 mindboggling designs. 52pp. 8¼ × 11.
24123-8 Pa. $2.75

PERSPECTIVE FOR ARTISTS, Rex Vicat Cole. Depth, perspective of sky and sea, shadows, much more, not usually covered. 391 diagrams, 81 reproductions of drawings and paintings. 279pp. 5⅜ × 8½.
22487-2 Pa. $4.00

MOVIE-STAR PORTRAITS OF THE FORTIES, edited by John Kobal. 163 glamor, studio photos of 106 stars of the 1940s: Rita Hayworth, Ava Gardner, Marlon Brando, Clark Gable, many more. 176pp. 8⅜ × 11¼.
23546-7 Pa. $6.95

STARS OF THE BROADWAY STAGE, 1940-1967, Fred Fehl. Marlon Brando, Uta Hagen, John Kerr, John Gielgud, Jessica Tandy in great shows—*South Pacific, Galileo, West Side Story*, more. 240 black-and-white photos. 144pp. 8⅜ × 11¼.
24398-2 Pa. $8.95

ILLUSTRATED DICTIONARY OF HISTORIC ARCHITECTURE, edited by Cyril M. Harris. Extraordinary compendium of clear, concise definitions for over 5000 important architectural terms complemented by over 2000 line drawings. 592pp. 7½ × 9⅜.
24444-X Pa. $14.95

THE EARLY WORK OF FRANK LLOYD WRIGHT, F.L. Wright. 207 rare photos of Oak Park period, first great buildings: Unity Temple, Dana house, Larkin factory. Complete photos of Wasmuth edition. New Introduction. 160pp. 8⅜ × 11¼.
24381-8 Pa. $7.95

LIVING MY LIFE, Emma Goldman. Candid, no holds barred account by foremost American anarchist: her own life, anarchist movement, famous contemporaries, ideas and their impact. 944pp. 5⅜ × 8½. 22543-7, 22544-5 Pa., Two-vol. set $13.00

UNDERSTANDING THERMODYNAMICS, H.C. Van Ness. Clear, lucid treatment of first and second laws of thermodynamics. Excellent supplement to basic textbook in undergraduate science or engineering class. 103pp. 5⅜ × 8.
63277-6 Pa. $5.50

SMOCKING: TECHNIQUE, PROJECTS, AND DESIGNS, Dianne Durand. Foremost smocking designer provides complete instructions on how to smock. Over 10 projects, over 100 illustrations. 56pp. 8¼ × 11. 23788-5 Pa. $2.00

AUDUBON'S BIRDS IN COLOR FOR DECOUPAGE, edited by Eleanor H. Rawlings. 24 sheets, 37 most decorative birds, full color, on one side of paper. Instructions, including work under glass. 56pp. 8¼ × 11. 23492-4 Pa. $3.95

THE COMPLETE BOOK OF SILK SCREEN PRINTING PRODUCTION, J.I. Biegeleisen. For commercial user, teacher in advanced classes, serious hobbyist. Most modern techniques, materials, equipment for optimal results. 124 illustrations. 253pp. 5⅜ × 8½. 21100-2 Pa. $4.50

A TREASURY OF ART NOUVEAU DESIGN AND ORNAMENT, edited by Carol Belanger Grafton. 577 designs for the practicing artist. Full-page, spots, borders, bookplates by Klimt, Bradley, others. 144pp. 8⅜ × 11¼. 24001-0 Pa. $5.95

ART NOUVEAU TYPOGRAPHIC ORNAMENTS, Dan X. Solo. Over 800 Art Nouveau florals, swirls, women, animals, borders, scrolls, wreaths, spots and dingbats, copyright-free. 100pp. 8⅛ × 11. 24366-4 Pa. $4.00

HAND SHADOWS TO BE THROWN UPON THE WALL, Henry Bursill. Wonderful Victorian novelty tells how to make flying birds, dog, goose, deer, and 14 others, each explained by a full-page illustration. 32pp. 6½ × 9¼. 21779-5 Pa. $1.50

AUDUBON'S BIRDS OF AMERICA COLORING BOOK, John James Audubon. Rendered for coloring by Paul Kennedy. 46 of Audubon's noted illustrations: red-wingèd black-bird, cardinal, etc. Original plates reproduced in full-color on the covers. Captions. 48pp. 8¼ × 11. 23049-X Pa. $2.25

SILK SCREEN TECHNIQUES, J.I. Biegeleisen, M.A. Cohn. Clear, practical, modern, economical. Minimal equipment (self-built), materials, easy methods. For amateur, hobbyist, 1st book. 141 illustrations. 185pp. 6⅛ × 9¼. 20433-2 Pa. $3.95

101 PATCHWORK PATTERNS, Ruby S. McKim. 101 beautiful, immediately useable patterns, full-size, modern and traditional. Also general information, estimating, quilt lore. 140 illustrations. 124pp. 7⅞ × 10¾. 20773-0 Pa. $3.50

READY-TO-USE FLORAL DESIGNS, Ed Sibbett, Jr. Over 100 floral designs (most in three sizes) of popular individual blossoms as well as bouquets, sprays, garlands. 64pp. 8¼ × 11. 23976-4 Pa. $2.95

AMERICAN WILD FLOWERS COLORING BOOK, Paul Kennedy. Planned coverage of 46 most important wildflowers, from Rickett's collection; instructive as well as entertaining. Color versions on covers. Captions. 48pp. 8¼ × 11. 20095-7 Pa. $2.50

CARVING DUCK DECOYS, Harry V. Shourds and Anthony Hillman. Detailed instructions and full-size templates for constructing 16 beautiful, marvelously practical decoys according to time-honored South Jersey method. 70pp. 9¼ × 12¼. 24083-5 Pa. $4.95

TRADITIONAL PATCHWORK PATTERNS, Carol Belanger Grafton. Cardboard cut-out pieces for use as templates to make 12 quilts: Buttercup, Ribbon Border, Tree of Paradise, nine more. Full instructions. 57pp. 8¼ × 11. 23015-5 Pa. $3.50

25 KITES THAT FLY, Leslie Hunt. Full, easy-to-follow instructions for kites made from inexpensive materials. Many novelties. 70 illustrations. 110pp. 5⅜ × 8½.
22550-X Pa. $2.25

PIANO TUNING, J. Cree Fischer. Clearest, best book for beginner, amateur. Simple repairs, raising dropped notes, tuning by easy method of flattened fifths. No previous skills needed. 4 illustrations. 201pp. 5⅜ × 8½. 23267-0 Pa. $3.50

EARLY AMERICAN IRON-ON TRANSFER PATTERNS, edited by Rita Weiss. 75 designs, borders, alphabets, from traditional American sources. 48pp. 8¼ × 11.
23162-3 Pa. $1.95

CROCHETING EDGINGS, edited by Rita Weiss. Over 100 of the best designs for these lovely trims for a host of household items. Complete instructions, illustrations. 48pp. 8¼ × 11. 24031-2 Pa. $2.25

FINGER PLAYS FOR NURSERY AND KINDERGARTEN, Emilie Poulsson. 18 finger plays with music (voice and piano); entertaining, instructive. Counting, nature lore, etc. Victorian classic. 53 illustrations. 80pp. 6½ × 9¼. 22588-7 Pa. $1.95

BOSTON THEN AND NOW, Peter Vanderwarker. Here in 59 side-by-side views are photographic documentations of the city's past and present. 119 photographs. Full captions. 122pp. 8¼ × 11. 24312-5 Pa. $6.95

CROCHETING BEDSPREADS, edited by Rita Weiss. 22 patterns, originally published in three instruction books 1939-41. 39 photos, 8 charts. Instructions. 48pp. 8¼ × 11. 23610-2 Pa. $2.00

HAWTHORNE ON PAINTING, Charles W. Hawthorne. Collected from notes taken by students at famous Cape Cod School; hundreds of direct, personal *apercus*, ideas, suggestions. 91pp. 5⅜ × 8½. 20653-X Pa. $2.50

THERMODYNAMICS, Enrico Fermi. A classic of modern science. Clear, organized treatment of systems, first and second laws, entropy, thermodynamic potentials, etc. Calculus required. 160pp. 5⅜ × 8½. 60361-X Pa. $4.00

TEN BOOKS ON ARCHITECTURE, Vitruvius. The most important book ever written on architecture. Early Roman aesthetics, technology, classical orders, site selection, all other aspects. Morgan translation. 331pp. 5⅜ × 8½. 20645-9 Pa. $5.50

THE CORNELL BREAD BOOK, Clive M. McCay and Jeanette B. McCay. Famed high-protein recipe incorporated into breads, rolls, buns, coffee cakes, pizza, pie crusts, more. Nearly 50 illustrations. 48pp. 8¼ × 11. 23995-0 Pa. $2.00

THE CRAFTSMAN'S HANDBOOK, Cennino Cennini. 15th-century handbook, school of Giotto, explains applying gold, silver leaf; gesso; fresco painting, grinding pigments, etc. 142pp. 6⅛ × 9¼. 20054-X Pa. $3.50

FRANK LLOYD WRIGHT'S FALLINGWATER, Donald Hoffmann. Full story of Wright's masterwork at Bear Run, Pa. 100 photographs of site, construction, and details of completed structure. 112pp. 9¼ × 10. 23671-4 Pa. $6.95

OVAL STAINED GLASS PATTERN BOOK, C. Eaton. 60 new designs framed in shape of an oval. Greater complexity, challenge with sinuous cats, birds, mandalas framed in antique shape. 64pp. 8¼ × 11. 24519-5 Pa. $3.50

CHILDREN'S BOOKPLATES AND LABELS, Ed Sibbett, Jr. 6 each of 12 types based on *Wizard of Oz, Alice,* nursery rhymes, fairy tales. Perforated; full color. 24pp. 8¼ × 11. 23538-6 Pa. $3.50

READY-TO-USE VICTORIAN COLOR STICKERS: 96 Pressure-Sensitive Seals, Carol Belanger Grafton. Drawn from authentic period sources. Motifs include heads of men, women, children, plus florals, animals, birds, more. Will adhere to any clean surface. 8pp. 8½ × 11. 24551-9 Pa. $2.95

CUT AND FOLD PAPER SPACESHIPS THAT FLY, Michael Grater. 16 colorful, easy-to-build spaceships that really fly. Star Shuttle, Lunar Freighter, Star Probe, 13 others. 32pp. 8¼ × 11. 23978-0 Pa. $2.50

CUT AND ASSEMBLE PAPER AIRPLANES THAT FLY, Arthur Baker. 8 aerodynamically sound, ready-to-build paper airplanes, designed with latest techniques. Fly *Pegasus, Daedalus, Songbird,* 5 other aircraft. Instructions. 32pp. 9¼ × 11¼. 24302-8 Pa. $3.95

SIDELIGHTS ON RELATIVITY, Albert Einstein. Two lectures delivered in 1920-21: *Ether and Relativity* and *Geometry and Experience.* Elegant ideas in non-mathematical form. 56pp. 5⅜ × 8½. 24511-X Pa. $2.25

FADS AND FALLACIES IN THE NAME OF SCIENCE, Martin Gardner. Fair, witty appraisal of cranks and quacks of science: Velikovsky, orgone energy, Bridey Murphy, medical fads, etc. 373pp. 5⅜ × 8½. 20394-8 Pa. $5.95

VACATION HOMES AND CABINS, U.S. Dept. of Agriculture. Complete plans for 16 cabins, vacation homes and other shelters. 105pp. 9 × 12. 23631-5 Pa. $4.95

HOW TO BUILD A WOOD-FRAME HOUSE, L.O. Anderson. Placement, foundations, framing, sheathing, roof, insulation, plaster, finishing—almost everything else. 179 illustrations. 223pp. 7⅞ × 10¾. 22954-8 Pa. $5.50

THE MYSTERY OF A HANSOM CAB, Fergus W. Hume. Bizarre murder in a hansom cab leads to engrossing investigation. Memorable characters, rich atmosphere. 19th-century bestseller, still enjoyable, exciting. 256pp. 5⅜ × 8. 21956-9 Pa. $4.00

MANUAL OF TRADITIONAL WOOD CARVING, edited by Paul N. Hasluck. Possibly the best book in English on the craft of wood carving. Practical instructions, along with 1,146 working drawings and photographic illustrations. 576pp. 6½ × 9¼. 23489-4 Pa. $8.95

WHITTLING AND WOODCARVING, E.J Tangerman. Best book on market; clear, full. If you can cut a potato, you can carve toys, puzzles, chains, etc. Over 464 illustrations. 293pp. 5⅜ × 8½. 20965-2 Pa. $4.95

AMERICAN TRADEMARK DESIGNS, Barbara Baer Capitman. 732 marks, logos and corporate-identity symbols. Categories include entertainment, heavy industry, food and beverage. All black-and-white in standard forms. 160pp. 8⅛ × 11. 23259-X Pa. $6.95

DECORATIVE FRAMES AND BORDERS, edited by Edmund V. Gillon, Jr. Largest collection of borders and frames ever compiled for use of artists and designers. Renaissance, neo-Greek, Art Nouveau, Art Deco, to mention only a few styles. 396 illustrations. 192pp. 8⅜ × 11¼. 22928-9 Pa. $6.00

CATALOG OF DOVER BOOKS

THE MURDER BOOK OF J.G. REEDER, Edgar Wallace. Eight suspenseful stories by bestselling mystery writer of 20s and 30s. Features the donnish Mr. J.G. Reeder of Public Prosecutor's Office. 128pp. 5⅜ × 8½. (Available in U.S. only)
24374-5 Pa. $3.50

ANNE ORR'S CHARTED DESIGNS, Anne Orr. Best designs by premier needlework designer, all on charts: flowers, borders, birds, children, alphabets, etc. Over 100 charts, 10 in color. Total of 40pp. 8¼ × 11. 23704-4 Pa. $2.50

BASIC CONSTRUCTION TECHNIQUES FOR HOUSES AND SMALL BUILDINGS SIMPLY EXPLAINED, U.S. Bureau of Naval Personnel. Grading, masonry, woodworking, floor and wall framing, roof framing, plastering, tile setting, much more. Over 675 illustrations. 568pp. 6½ × 9¼. 20242-9 Pa. $8.95

MATISSE LINE DRAWINGS AND PRINTS, Henri Matisse. Representative collection of female nudes, faces, still lifes, experimental works, etc., from 1898 to 1948. 50 illustrations. 48pp. 8⅜ × 11¼. 23877-6 Pa. $2.50

HOW TO PLAY THE CHESS OPENINGS, Eugene Znosko-Borovsky. Clear, profound examinations of just what each opening is intended to do and how opponent can counter. Many sample games. 147pp. 5⅜ × 8½. 22795-2 Pa. $2.95

DUPLICATE BRIDGE, Alfred Sheinwold. Clear, thorough, easily followed account: rules, etiquette, scoring, strategy, bidding; Goren's point-count system, Blackwood and Gerber conventions, etc. 158pp. 5⅜ × 8½. 22741-3 Pa. $3.00

SARGENT PORTRAIT DRAWINGS, J.S. Sargent. Collection of 42 portraits reveals technical skill and intuitive eye of noted American portrait painter, John Singer Sargent. 48pp. 8¼ × 11⅛. 24524-1 Pa. $2.95

ENTERTAINING SCIENCE EXPERIMENTS WITH EVERYDAY OBJECTS, Martin Gardner. Over 100 experiments for youngsters. Will amuse, astonish, teach, and entertain. Over 100 illustrations. 127pp. 5⅜ × 8½. 24201-3 Pa. $2.50

TEDDY BEAR PAPER DOLLS IN FULL COLOR: A Family of Four Bears and Their Costumes, Crystal Collins. A family of four Teddy Bear paper dolls and nearly 60 cut-out costumes. Full color, printed one side only. 32pp. 9¼ × 12¼.
24550-0 Pa. $3.50

NEW CALLIGRAPHIC ORNAMENTS AND FLOURISHES, Arthur Baker. Unusual, multi-useable material: arrows, pointing hands, brackets and frames, ovals, swirls, birds, etc. Nearly 700 illustrations. 80pp. 8⅜ × 11¼.
24095-9 Pa. $3.75

DINOSAUR DIORAMAS TO CUT & ASSEMBLE, M. Kalmenoff. Two complete three-dimensional scenes in full color, with 31 cut-out animals and plants. Excellent educational toy for youngsters. Instructions; 2 assembly diagrams. 32pp. 9¼ × 12¼. 24541-1 Pa. $4.50

SILHOUETTES: A PICTORIAL ARCHIVE OF VARIED ILLUSTRATIONS, edited by Carol Belanger Grafton. Over 600 silhouettes from the 18th to 20th centuries. Profiles and full figures of men, women, children, birds, animals, groups and scenes, nature, ships, an alphabet. 144pp. 8⅜ × 11¼. 23781-8 Pa. $4.95

SURREAL STICKERS AND UNREAL STAMPS, William Rowe. 224 haunting, hilarious stamps on gummed, perforated stock, with images of elephants, geisha girls, George Washington, etc. 16pp. one side. 8¼ × 11. 24371-0 Pa. $3.50

GOURMET KITCHEN LABELS, Ed Sibbett, Jr. 112 full-color labels (4 copies each of 28 designs). Fruit, bread, other culinary motifs. Gummed and perforated. 16pp. 8¼ × 11. 24087-8 Pa. $2.95

PATTERNS AND INSTRUCTIONS FOR CARVING AUTHENTIC BIRDS, H.D. Green. Detailed instructions, 27 diagrams, 85 photographs for carving 15 species of birds so life-like, they'll seem ready to fly! 8¼ × 11. 24222-6 Pa. $2.75

FLATLAND, E.A. Abbott. Science-fiction classic explores life of 2-D being in 3-D world. 16 illustrations. 103pp. 5⅜ × 8. 20001-9 Pa. $2.00

DRIED FLOWERS, Sarah Whitlock and Martha Rankin. Concise, clear, practical guide to dehydration, glycerinizing, pressing plant material, and more. Covers use of silica gel. 12 drawings. 32pp. 5⅜ × 8½. 21802-3 Pa. $1.00

EASY-TO-MAKE CANDLES, Gary V. Guy. Learn how easy it is to make all kinds of decorative candles. Step-by-step instructions. 82 illustrations. 48pp. 8¼ × 11.
23881-4 Pa. $2.50

SUPER STICKERS FOR KIDS, Carolyn Bracken. 128 gummed and perforated full-color stickers: GIRL WANTED, KEEP OUT, BORED OF EDUCATION, X-RATED, COMBAT ZONE, many others. 16pp. 8¼ × 11. 24092-4 Pa. $2.50

CUT AND COLOR PAPER MASKS, Michael Grater. Clowns, animals, funny faces...simply color them in, cut them out, and put them together, and you have 9 paper masks to play with and enjoy. 32pp. 8¼ × 11. 23171-2 Pa. $2.25

A CHRISTMAS CAROL: THE ORIGINAL MANUSCRIPT, Charles Dickens. Clear facsimile of Dickens manuscript, on facing pages with final printed text. 8 illustrations by John Leech, 4 in color on covers. 144pp. 8⅜ × 11¼.
20980-6 Pa. $5.95

CARVING SHOREBIRDS, Harry V. Shourds & Anthony Hillman. 16 full-size patterns (all double-page spreads) for 19 North American shorebirds with step-by-step instructions. 72pp. 9¼ × 12¼. 24287-0 Pa. $4.95

THE GENTLE ART OF MATHEMATICS, Dan Pedoe. Mathematical games, probability, the question of infinity, topology, how the laws of algebra work, problems of irrational numbers, and more. 42 figures. 143pp. 5⅜ × 8½. (EBE)
22949-1 Pa. $3.50

READY-TO-USE DOLLHOUSE WALLPAPER, Katzenbach & Warren, Inc. Stripe, 2 floral stripes, 2 allover florals, polka dot; all in full color. 4 sheets (350 sq. in.) of each, enough for average room. 48pp. 8¼ × 11. 23495-9 Pa. $2.95

MINIATURE IRON-ON TRANSFER PATTERNS FOR DOLLHOUSES, DOLLS, AND SMALL PROJECTS, Rita Weiss and Frank Fontana. Over 100 miniature patterns: rugs, bedspreads, quilts, chair seats, etc. In standard dollhouse size. 48pp. 8¼ × 11. 23741-9 Pa. $1.95

THE DINOSAUR COLORING BOOK, Anthony Rao. 45 renderings of dinosaurs, fossil birds, turtles, other creatures of Mesozoic Era. Scientifically accurate. Captions. 48pp. 8¼ × 11. 24022-3 Pa. $2.50

THE BOOK OF WOOD CARVING, Charles Marshall Sayers. Still finest book for beginning student. Fundamentals, technique; gives 34 designs, over 34 projects for panels, bookends, mirrors, etc. 33 photos. 118pp. 7¾ × 10⅝. 23654-4 Pa. $3.95

CARVING COUNTRY CHARACTERS, Bill Higginbotham. Expert advice for beginning, advanced carvers on materials, techniques for creating 18 projects—mirthful panorama of American characters. 105 illustrations. 80pp. 8⅜ × 11.
24135-1 Pa. $2.50

300 ART NOUVEAU DESIGNS AND MOTIFS IN FULL COLOR, C.B. Grafton. 44 full-page plates display swirling lines and muted colors typical of Art Nouveau. Borders, frames, panels, cartouches, dingbats, etc. 48pp. 9⅜ × 12¼.
24354-0 Pa. $6.95

SELF-WORKING CARD TRICKS, Karl Fulves. Editor of *Pallbearer* offers 72 tricks that work automatically through nature of card deck. No sleight of hand needed. Often spectacular. 42 illustrations. 113pp. 5⅜ × 8½. 23334-0 Pa. $3.50

CUT AND ASSEMBLE A WESTERN FRONTIER TOWN, Edmund V. Gillon, Jr. Ten authentic full-color buildings on heavy cardboard stock in H-O scale. Sheriff's Office and Jail, Saloon, Wells Fargo, Opera House, others. 48pp. 9¼ × 12¼.
23736-2 Pa. $3.95

CUT AND ASSEMBLE AN EARLY NEW ENGLAND VILLAGE, Edmund V. Gillon, Jr. Printed in full color on heavy cardboard stock. 12 authentic buildings in H-O scale: Adams home in Quincy, Mass., Oliver Wight house in Sturbridge, smithy, store, church, others. 48pp. 9¼ × 12¼. 23536-X Pa. $4.95

THE TALE OF TWO BAD MICE, Beatrix Potter. Tom Thumb and Hunca Munca squeeze out of their hole and go exploring. 27 full-color Potter illustrations. 59pp. 4¼ × 5½. (Available in U.S. only) 23065-1 Pa. $1.75

CARVING FIGURE CARICATURES IN THE OZARK STYLE, Harold L. Enlow. Instructions and illustrations for ten delightful projects, plus general carving instructions. 22 drawings and 47 photographs altogether. 39pp. 8⅜ × 11.
23151-8 Pa. $2.50

A TREASURY OF FLOWER DESIGNS FOR ARTISTS, EMBROIDERERS AND CRAFTSMEN, Susan Gaber. 100 garden favorites lushly rendered by artist for artists, craftsmen, needleworkers. Many form frames, borders. 80pp. 8¼ × 11.
24096-7 Pa. $3.50

CUT & ASSEMBLE A TOY THEATER/THE NUTCRACKER BALLET, Tom Tierney. Model of a complete, full-color production of Tchaikovsky's classic. 6 backdrops, dozens of characters, familiar dance sequences. 32pp. 9⅜ × 12¼.
24194-7 Pa. $4.50

ANIMALS: 1,419 COPYRIGHT-FREE ILLUSTRATIONS OF MAMMALS, BIRDS, FISH, INSECTS, ETC., edited by Jim Harter. Clear wood engravings present, in extremely lifelike poses, over 1,000 species of animals. 284pp. 9 × 12.
23766-4 Pa. $9.95

MORE HAND SHADOWS, Henry Bursill. For those at their 'finger ends," 16 more effects—Shakespeare, a hare, a squirrel, Mr. Punch, and twelve more—each explained by a full-page illustration. Considerable period charm. 30pp. 6½ × 9¼.
21384-6 Pa. $1.95

CHANCERY CURSIVE STROKE BY STROKE, Arthur Baker. Instructions and illustrations for each stroke of each letter (upper and lower case) and numerals. 54 full-page plates. 64pp. 8¼ × 11. 24278-1 Pa. $2.50

THE ENJOYMENT AND USE OF COLOR, Walter Sargent. Color relationships, values, intensities; complementary colors, illumination, similar topics. Color in nature and art. 7 color plates, 29 illustrations. 274pp. 5⅜ × 8½. 20944-X Pa. $4.95

SCULPTURE PRINCIPLES AND PRACTICE, Louis Slobodkin. Step-by-step approach to clay, plaster, metals, stone; classical and modern. 253 drawings, photos. 255pp. 8⅛ × 11. 22960-2 Pa. $7.50

VICTORIAN FASHION PAPER DOLLS FROM HARPER'S BAZAR, 1867-1898, Theodore Menten. Four female dolls with 28 elegant high fashion costumes, printed in full color. 32pp. 9¼ × 12¼. 23453-3 Pa. $3.50

FLOPSY, MOPSY AND COTTONTAIL: A Little Book of Paper Dolls in Full Color, Susan LaBelle. Three dolls and 21 costumes (7 for each doll) show Peter Rabbit's siblings dressed for holidays, gardening, hiking, etc. Charming borders, captions. 48pp. 4¼ × 5½. 24376-1 Pa. $2.25

NATIONAL LEAGUE BASEBALL CARD CLASSICS, Bert Randolph Sugar. 83 big-leaguers from 1909-69 on facsimile cards. Hubbell, Dean, Spahn, Brock plus advertising, info, no duplications. Perforated, detachable. 16pp. 8¼ × 11.
24308-7 Pa. $2.95

THE LOGICAL APPROACH TO CHESS, Dr. Max Euwe, et al. First-rate text of comprehensive strategy, tactics, theory for the amateur. No gambits to memorize, just a clear, logical approach. 224pp. 5⅜ × 8½. 24353-2 Pa. $4.50

MAGICK IN THEORY AND PRACTICE, Aleister Crowley. The summation of the thought and practice of the century's most famous necromancer, long hard to find. Crowley's best book. 436pp. 5⅜ × 8½. (Available in U.S. only)
23295-6 Pa. $6.50

THE HAUNTED HOTEL, Wilkie Collins. Collins' last great tale; doom and destiny in a Venetian palace. Praised by T.S. Eliot. 127pp. 5⅜ × 8½.
24333-8 Pa. $3.00

ART DECO DISPLAY ALPHABETS, Dan X. Solo. Wide variety of bold yet elegant lettering in handsome Art Deco styles. 100 complete fonts, with numerals, punctuation, more. 104pp. 8⅛ × 11. 24372-9 Pa. $4.50

CALLIGRAPHIC ALPHABETS, Arthur Baker. Nearly 150 complete alphabets by outstanding contemporary. Stimulating ideas; useful source for unique effects. 154 plates. 157pp. 8⅜ × 11¼. 21045-6 Pa. $5.95

ARTHUR BAKER'S HISTORIC CALLIGRAPHIC ALPHABETS, Arthur Baker. From monumental capitals of first-century Rome to humanistic cursive of 16th century, 33 alphabets in fresh interpretations. 88 plates. 96pp. 9 × 12.
24054-1 Pa. $4.50

LETTIE LANE PAPER DOLLS, Sheila Young. Genteel turn-of-the-century family very popular then and now. 24 paper dolls. 16 plates in full color. 32pp. 9¼ × 12¼. 24089-4 Pa. $3.50

TWENTY-FOUR ART NOUVEAU POSTCARDS IN FULL COLOR FROM CLASSIC POSTERS, Hayward and Blanche Cirker. Ready-to-mail postcards reproduced from rare set of poster art. Works by Toulouse-Lautrec, Parrish, Steinlen, Mucha, Cheret, others. 12pp. 8¼× 11. 24389-3 Pa. $2.95

READY-TO-USE ART NOUVEAU BOOKMARKS IN FULL COLOR, Carol Belanger Grafton. 30 elegant bookmarks featuring graceful, flowing lines, foliate motifs, sensuous women characteristic of Art Nouveau. Perforated for easy detaching. 16pp. 8¼ × 11. 24305-2 Pa. $2.95

FRUIT KEY AND TWIG KEY TO TREES AND SHRUBS, William M. Harlow. Fruit key covers 120 deciduous and evergreen species; twig key covers 160 deciduous species. Easily used. Over 300 photographs. 126pp. 5⅜ × 8½. 20511-8 Pa. $2.25

LEONARDO DRAWINGS, Leonardo da Vinci. Plants, landscapes, human face and figure, etc., plus studies for Sforza monument, *Last Supper*, more. 60 illustrations. 64pp. 8¼ × 11⅛. 23951-9 Pa. $2.75

CLASSIC BASEBALL CARDS, edited by Bert R. Sugar. 98 classic cards on heavy stock, full color, perforated for detaching. Ruth, Cobb, Durocher, DiMaggio, H. Wagner, 99 others. Rare originals cost hundreds. 16pp. 8¼ × 11. 23498-3 Pa. $3.25

TREES OF THE EASTERN AND CENTRAL UNITED STATES AND CANADA, William M. Harlow. Best one-volume guide to 140 trees. Full descriptions, woodlore, range, etc. Over 600 illustrations. Handy size. 288pp. 4½ × 6⅜. 20395-6 Pa. $3.95

JUDY GARLAND PAPER DOLLS IN FULL COLOR, Tom Tierney. 3 Judy Garland paper dolls (teenager, grown-up, and mature woman) and 30 gorgeous costumes highlighting memorable career. Captions. 32pp. 9¼ × 12¼.

24404-0 Pa. $3.50

GREAT FASHION DESIGNS OF THE BELLE EPOQUE PAPER DOLLS IN FULL COLOR, Tom Tierney. Two dolls and 30 costumes meticulously rendered. Haute couture by Worth, Lanvin, Paquin, other greats late Victorian to WWI. 32pp. 9¼ × 12¼. 24425-3 Pa. $3.50

FASHION PAPER DOLLS FROM GODEY'S LADY'S BOOK, 1840-1854, Susan Johnston. In full color: 7 female fashion dolls with 50 costumes. Little girl's, bridal, riding, bathing, wedding, evening, everyday, etc. 32pp. 9¼ × 12¼.

23511-4 Pa. $3.95

THE BOOK OF THE SACRED MAGIC OF ABRAMELIN THE MAGE, translated by S. MacGregor Mathers. Medieval manuscript of ceremonial magic. Basic document in Aleister Crowley, Golden Dawn groups. 268pp. 5⅜ × 8½.

23211-5 Pa. $5.00

PETER RABBIT POSTCARDS IN FULL COLOR: 24 Ready-to-Mail Cards, Susan Whited LaBelle. Bunnies ice-skating, coloring Easter eggs, making valentines, many other charming scenes. 24 perforated full-color postcards, each measuring 4¼ × 6, on coated stock. 12pp. 9 × 12. 24617-5 Pa. $2.95

CELTIC HAND STROKE BY STROKE, A. Baker. Complete guide creating each letter of the alphabet in distinctive Celtic manner. Covers hand position, strokes, pens, inks, paper, more. Illustrated. 48pp. 8¼ × 11. 24336-2 Pa. $2.50

DECORATIVE NAPKIN FOLDING FOR BEGINNERS, Lillian Oppenheimer and Natalie Epstein. 22 different napkin folds in the shape of a heart, clown's hat, love knot, etc. 63 drawings. 48pp. 8¼ × 11. 23797-4 Pa. $1.95

DECORATIVE LABELS FOR HOME CANNING, PRESERVING, AND OTHER HOUSEHOLD AND GIFT USES, Theodore Menten. 128 gummed, perforated labels, beautifully printed in 2 colors. 12 versions. Adhere to metal, glass, wood, ceramics. 24pp. 8¼ × 11. 23219-0 Pa. $2.95

EARLY AMERICAN STENCILS ON WALLS AND FURNITURE, Janet Waring. Thorough coverage of 19th-century folk art: techniques, artifacts, surviving specimens. 166 illustrations, 7 in color. 147pp. of text. 7⅞ × 10¾. 21906-2 Pa. $9.95

AMERICAN ANTIQUE WEATHERVANES, A.B. & W.T. Westervelt. Extensively illustrated 1883 catalog exhibiting over 550 copper weathervanes and finials. Excellent primary source by one of the principal manufacturers. 104pp. 6⅛ × 9¼. 24396-6 Pa. $3.95

ART STUDENTS' ANATOMY, Edmond J. Farris. Long favorite in art schools. Basic elements, common positions, actions. Full text, 158 illustrations. 159pp. 5⅜ × 8½. 20744-7 Pa. $3.95

BRIDGMAN'S LIFE DRAWING, George B. Bridgman. More than 500 drawings and text teach you to abstract the body into its major masses. Also specific areas of anatomy. 192pp. 6½ × 9¼. (EA) 22710-3 Pa. $4.50

COMPLETE PRELUDES AND ETUDES FOR SOLO PIANO, Frederic Chopin. All 26 Preludes, all 27 Etudes by greatest composer of piano music. Authoritative Paderewski edition. 224pp. 9 × 12. (Available in U.S. only) 24052-5 Pa. $7.50

PIANO MUSIC 1888-1905, Claude Debussy. Deux Arabesques, Suite Bergamesque, Masques, 1st series of Images, etc. 9 others, in corrected editions. 175pp. 9⅜ × 12¼. (ECE) 22771-5 Pa. $5.95

TEDDY BEAR IRON-ON TRANSFER PATTERNS, Ted Menten. 80 iron-on transfer patterns of male and female Teddys in a wide variety of activities, poses, sizes. 48pp. 8¼ × 11. 24596-9 Pa. $2.25

A PICTURE HISTORY OF THE BROOKLYN BRIDGE, M.J. Shapiro. Profusely illustrated account of greatest engineering achievement of 19th century. 167 rare photos & engravings recall construction, human drama. Extensive, detailed text. 122pp. 8¼ × 11. 24403-2 Pa. $7.95

NEW YORK IN THE THIRTIES, Berenice Abbott. Noted photographer's fascinating study shows new buildings that have become famous and old sights that have disappeared forever. 97 photographs. 97pp. 11⅜ × 10. 22967-X Pa. $7.50

MATHEMATICAL TABLES AND FORMULAS, Robert D. Carmichael and Edwin R. Smith. Logarithms, sines, tangents, trig functions, powers, roots, reciprocals, exponential and hyperbolic functions, formulas and theorems. 269pp. 5⅜ × 8½. 60111-0 Pa. $4.95

HANDBOOK OF MATHEMATICAL FUNCTIONS WITH FORMULAS, GRAPHS, AND MATHEMATICAL TABLES, edited by Milton Abramowitz and Irene A. Stegun. Vast compendium: 29 sets of tables, some to as high as 20 places. 1,046pp. 8 × 10½. 61272-4 Pa. $19.95

YUCATAN BEFORE AND AFTER THE CONQUEST, Diego de Landa. Only significant account of Yucatan written in the early post-Conquest era. Translated by William Gates. Over 120 illustrations. 162pp. 5⅜ × 8½. 23622-6 Pa. $3.50

ORNATE PICTORIAL CALLIGRAPHY, E.A. Lupfer. Complete instructions, over 150 examples help you create magnificent "flourishes" from which beautiful animals and objects gracefully emerge. 8⅛ × 11. 21957-7 Pa. $2.95

DOLLY DINGLE PAPER DOLLS, Grace Drayton. Cute chubby children by same artist who did Campbell Kids. Rare plates from 1910s. 30 paper dolls and over 100 outfits reproduced in full color. 32pp. 9¼ × 12¼. 23711-7 Pa. $3.50

CURIOUS GEORGE PAPER DOLLS IN FULL COLOR, H. A. Rey, Kathy Allert. Naughty little monkey-hero of children's books in two doll figures, plus 48 full-color costumes: pirate, Indian chief, fireman, more. 32pp. 9¼ × 12¼. 24386-9 Pa. $3.50

GERMAN: HOW TO SPEAK AND WRITE IT, Joseph Rosenberg. Like *French, How to Speak and Write It*. Very rich modern course, with a wealth of pictorial material. 330 illustrations. 384pp. 5⅜ × 8½. (USUKO) 20271-2 Pa. $4.75

CATS AND KITTENS: 24 Ready-to-Mail Color Photo Postcards, D. Holby. Handsome collection; feline in a variety of adorable poses. Identifications. 12pp. on postcard stock. 8¼ × 11. 24469-5 Pa. $2.95

MARILYN MONROE PAPER DOLLS, Tom Tierney. 31 full-color designs on heavy stock, from *The Asphalt Jungle, Gentlemen Prefer Blondes,* 22 others. 1 doll. 16 plates. 32pp. 9⅜ × 12¼. 23769-9 Pa. $3.50

FUNDAMENTALS OF LAYOUT, F.H. Wills. All phases of layout design discussed and illustrated in 121 illustrations. Indispensable as student's text or handbook for professional. 124pp. 8⅛ × 11. 21279-3 Pa. $4.50

FANTASTIC SUPER STICKERS, Ed Sibbett, Jr. 75 colorful pressure-sensitive stickers. Peel off and place for a touch of pizzazz: clowns, penguins, teddy bears, etc. Full color. 16pp. 8¼ × 11. 24471-7 Pa. $2.95

LABELS FOR ALL OCCASIONS, Ed Sibbett, Jr. 6 labels each of 16 different designs—baroque, art nouveau, art deco, Pennsylvania Dutch, etc.—in full color. 24pp. 8¼ × 11. 23688-9 Pa. $2.95

HOW TO CALCULATE QUICKLY: RAPID METHODS IN BASIC MATHEMATICS, Henry Sticker. Addition, subtraction, multiplication, division, checks, etc. More than 8000 problems, solutions. 185pp. 5 × 7¼. 20295-X Pa. $2.95

THE CAT COLORING BOOK, Karen Baldauski. Handsome, realistic renderings of 40 splendid felines, from American shorthair to exotic types. 44 plates. Captions. 48pp. 8¼ × 11. 24011-8 Pa. $2.25

THE TALE OF PETER RABBIT, Beatrix Potter. The inimitable Peter's terrifying adventure in Mr. McGregor's garden, with all 27 wonderful, full-color Potter illustrations. 55pp. 4¼ × 5½. (Available in U.S. only) 22827-4 Pa. $1.75

BASIC ELECTRICITY, U.S. Bureau of Naval Personnel. Batteries, circuits, conductors, AC and DC, inductance and capacitance, generators, motors, transformers, amplifiers, etc. 349 illustrations. 448pp. 6½ × 9¼. 20973-3 Pa. $7.95

SOURCE BOOK OF MEDICAL HISTORY, edited by Logan Clendening, M.D. Original accounts ranging from Ancient Egypt and Greece to discovery of X-rays: Galen, Pasteur, Lavoisier, Harvey, Parkinson, others. 685pp. 5⅜ × 8½.
20621-1 Pa. $10.95

THE ROSE AND THE KEY, J.S. Lefanu. Superb mystery novel from Irish master. Dark doings among an ancient and aristocratic English family. Well-drawn characters; capital suspense. Introduction by N. Donaldson. 448pp. 5⅜ × 8½.
24377-X Pa. $6.95

SOUTH WIND, Norman Douglas. Witty, elegant novel of ideas set on languorous Mediterranean island of Nepenthe. Elegant prose, glittering epigrams, mordant satire. 1917 masterpiece. 416pp. 5⅜ × 8½. (Available in U.S. only)
24361-3 Pa. $5.95

RUSSELL'S CIVIL WAR PHOTOGRAPHS, Capt. A.J. Russell. 116 rare Civil War Photos: Bull Run, Virginia campaigns, bridges, railroads, Richmond, Lincoln's funeral car. Many never seen before. Captions. 128pp. 9⅜ × 12¼.
24283-8 Pa. $6.95

PHOTOGRAPHS BY MAN RAY: 105 Works, 1920-1934. Nudes, still lifes, landscapes, women's faces, celebrity portraits (Dali, Matisse, Picasso, others), rayographs. Reprinted from rare gravure edition. 128pp. 9⅜ × 12¼. (Available in U.S. only)
23842-3 Pa. $7.95

STAR NAMES: THEIR LORE AND MEANING, Richard H. Allen. Star names, the zodiac, constellations: folklore and literature associated with heavens. The basic book of its field, fascinating reading. 563pp. 5⅜ × 8½.
21079-0 Pa. $7.95

BURNHAM'S CELESTIAL HANDBOOK, Robert Burnham, Jr. Thorough guide to the stars beyond our solar system. Exhaustive treatment. Alphabetical by constellation: Andromeda to Cetus in Vol. 1; Chamaeleon to Orion in Vol. 2; and Pavo to Vulpecula in Vol. 3. Hundreds of illustrations. Index in Vol. 3. 2000pp. 6⅛ × 9¼.
23567-X, 23568-8, 23673-0 Pa. Three-vol. set $36.85

THE ART NOUVEAU STYLE BOOK OF ALPHONSE MUCHA, Alphonse Mucha. All 72 plates from *Documents Decoratifs* in original color. Stunning, essential work of Art Nouveau. 80pp. 9⅜ × 12¼.
24044-4 Pa. $7.95

DESIGNS BY ERTE; FASHION DRAWINGS AND ILLUSTRATIONS FROM "HARPER'S BAZAR," Erte. 310 fabulous line drawings and 14 *Harper's Bazar* covers, 8 in full color. Erte's exotic temptresses with tassels, fur muffs, long trains, coifs, more. 129pp. 9⅜ × 12¼.
23397-9 Pa. $6.95

HISTORY OF STRENGTH OF MATERIALS, Stephen P. Timoshenko. Excellent historical survey of the strength of materials with many references to the theories of elasticity and structure. 245 figures. 452pp. 5⅜ × 8½. 61187-6 Pa. $8.95